# THE CORNER OF EAST AND DREAMS

## JOAN CONNOR

RUNNING
*Wild*
PRESS

*The Corner of East and Dreams*
text copyright © Reserved by Joan Connor
Edited by Barbara Lockwood

Front Cover Image by Robert Waldo Brunelle, Jr.
It was painted in 2017.
Cover Image title: The Pierce Building, Rutland 1850

Paperback ISBN: 978-1-955062-26-8
eBook ISBN: 978-1-955062-27-5

# CONTENTS

*This collection is dedicated to the memory of my friend John Michael Drew.*

# THE PAINBROKER

S he walked through the evening streets. The cobbles and bricks, the stone and iron grillwork, the very air itself seemed washed in sepia. A yellow moon moaned through the fog.

What had she left to pawn? A lock of hair? A gold watch? A tortoiseshell comb? A fob? Her walls and floors were bare. Only her clothes remained her, her drab dress, the shawl which she wound around her against the fog. But she could offer the shawl.

She turned into the alleyway, her shoulder following the wall, and rapped on the unpainted Dutch door. The top of the door swung to, and she peered in. "Please," she said.

The top of the door closed again, and she heard a jangle of keys. "Come in," the pawnbroker said and he trundled back to his stool behind the counter grille.

The close room smelled of onion and damp rags, unredeemed wedding rings and gun oil, despair and wax, small coin and kerosene from the guttering flame which licked sootily at its chimney and seesawed the room in queasy yellow light.

1

"What is it?" the pawnbroker asked. He squinted at her and snuffled, a dog keen on a scent.

"There is little left," she said, fanning out her shawl. But it was a fine shawl, cashmere, from him, the one she sought to please, for him now. A little pilled and linty.

"I will not take your wrap," the pawnbroker said.

"Please."

"No. I do not want it."

He raised the lamp so she could regard his face. But she could never read his eyes. They were dimpled in his face like thumbholes in dough, his eyebrows scalloping over them, their fleshy festoons. He spoke from some dark, enfolded space which she could not see. The yellow light flickered over his bald pate. His hands raised the lamp higher, and she could see the stumps. Missing ring-fingers.

She'd inquired about them once, gently. His mouth twisted into a möbius band, a smile, a frown, both. "I pawned them."

He was her last fear; all the others she had released leaf by leaf, stripping herself down to a sapling, an essential nakedness of want, a singular want. She searched for his eyes in the deep sockets, but not finding them, lowered her own.

The pawnbroker laughed, a dry laugh, the papery sound of bat's wings. "Do you think he is worth it, this man for whom you pawn your pots and pans, your boots, your books, your heart?"

"How did you know?" she whispered.

The yellow tongues licked his shiny forehead. He clucked his tongue. "Because you saved the ring till last. The shawl." He picked up the pinky ring from the case on the counter and rolled it between thumb and forefinger. "Round and round, it rolls and rolls." His laugh flittered again.

She cringed as it passed her.

"I will not take your shawl," he said.

She nodded, tightened the shawl about her. "Then I shall go."

"Stay." He lifted the lamp. "You have something else I will accept."

She extended her empty palms before her and shook her head. "This is my fortune." She watched him, and for a moment she thought that she heard a rustle, glimpsed something, someone behind him move -- a cinched waist, the bell of a gown. But perhaps it was just the light mocking her, the flame chuckling softly, the shadows congregating and dispersing.

"Your pain," he said and grinned.

She took a step backward, catching her heel on a heap of rags. She righted herself. "What do you mean?"

"Your pain. You carry so much. Pawn it. Come here," he said and leaned his head toward the grate.

He looked for the moment like a figure in a puppet show. Punch, jailed. A cast of silhouettes behind him. The shadows whispered. She stepped forward and, closer to him now, she could smell the onions on his breath, the acetic rot of wine, claret perhaps. Surely red; it wounded his breath and bloodied his lips. But his cheeks, by this light, were unstubbled. He had the skin of a pear, a white one, aberrant.

Wine, onion, pear, dough, he made her think of food, and her stomach opened in her an empty larder. He clinked three gold coins on the counter, then pushed out the pinky ring beneath the grille with his stub. "There. Take them. They are yours. All for the burden of your pain. A fair exchange. A fair exchange."

Her heart and stomach hollowed with want. The coins could purchase bread and perhaps a new coat for him, the one she loved, he who would not leave his wife. Yes, but it seemed an unfair trade. "How?" she asked. "How do I leave my pain?"

"Merely assent." He smiled a small coaxing smile. "You will be the better for it."

She stepped forward and retrieved the three gold coins, leaving the ring. "Done then."

"Done," he said. And she thought she saw behind him a woman's face, pale but with red lips, flushed cheeks. She shook her head, a trick of light, and turned to leave.

On the street the three coins felt heavier in her hand. Had he tricked her or she him? She could not know, but if she had swapped her pain, shouldn't she feel lighter now, shouldn't she have forgotten him? But she always carried him with her. He was with her now; she knew no respite. What then had her pact with the pawnbroker been? Out of habit she rubbed the base of her pinkie with her thumb, an absent gesture. Absence could be more present than presence. A missing ring, a token habit.

The fog shredded as if a comb had been drawn through it. Shapes emerged from the misty tendrils. A woman skulked past her, stinking of gin, medicinal and junipery. As the woman passed her, she drew sharp breath, stabbed by her sadness. She saw the woman's three infants, swaddled and dead in her arms. The vision shimmered, then disappeared like fog. For a moment she wanted to go to the woman, to console her, but the woman lurched ahead into the ribbony fog.

A bicycle approached her. A boy's startled face parting the night. She smiled at him and, even as she smiled, she saw bruises mottle his face, a welt rise on his brow, heard his father's voice braying with port and laughter.

And then she knew. The coins weighed heavily with their price. They were her pawn ticket and she the pawnbroker's pawn. She had contracted to know the private pains of others, their griefs and losses, their beatings, their sleeved bruises.

And as she walked back to her room in the abandoned

warehouse by the piers, she saw them all: the gambled fortunes, the unfaithful spouses, the gnawing hungers, the disappointed loves, the daughters who endured their shame privately, and suffered disproportionately except, except. It was, none of it, disproportionate. No one was spared. All bore their pains, and then she knew that life was pain. And she could live with this knowledge of the condition of life, but she could not live with the details.

Perhaps it was not too late to rescind her exchange with the pawnbroker. She would buy back her pain with the three coins grown heavier with each sorrow until her arm ached with the weight, dragging it like an anchor.

She curled into her corner, wrapped herself in her shawl and waited for morning. In the port the foghorns mourned, and moonlight gashed the floor by her feet through the jagged windowpane. She could not sleep so she rehearsed what she would tell the pawnbroker when she returned his three coins. It made her tranquil, more tranquil than sleep.

A jag of sunlight replaced the jag of moonlight. So, she had fallen asleep. She opened her palm. The three coins still nested there, and she arranged her hair in her broken reflection in the pane, draped her shawl and set off for the broker's.

As she passed the sailors and vendors in the morning streets, she averted her eyes so that their secret trials would not trouble her. She had only this thought: to return to the broker's and reclaim her pain. But the aroma of bread in a bakery taunted her until she quailed before her hunger. She set one heavy coin on the counter, and the baker regarded it and her with squinted eyes. He bit the coin.

His webby sadness reached for her. A daughter whom he had banished but a week dead, her fatherless, now motherless baby at home with the baker's wife.

"A cinnamon loaf, please," she said.

He wrapped the loaf in paper and made change.

"I am sorry about your daughter," she said, eyes downcast as she accepted the loaf.

As soon as her feet struck the pavement, she let the paper flutter away and fell upon the loaf, sparing not a crumb. She did not taste it. Sores formed on the roof of her mouth – she had been a long time without food – but still she ate, ripped chunks of bread with her greedy teeth. It hurt to swallow.

When she finished, she noted that her left hand felt lighter now with one coin gone. Not as light as the ringless hand, but lighter nonetheless. She glanced up then and saw the coat in the storefront, the coat that she had wanted for him, thinking how handsome he would look in it, how warm he would be when fog gave way to snow.

She approached the window. The coat was wool, vaguely military in cut, a nipped waist, flared tails, full in length. It was worn, but barely. The fabric, sturdy and thick, had stood up to its wearer. A deep blue, the coat was almost black. Gold buttons glittered starlike on the wool. The coins jingled.

She ducked into the shop. The room was thick with dust and rummage. "Please," she said, "I'd like the coat."

"It would be far too large for you," the clerk answered, posing with a bedraggled feather duster, more accessory than utile.

A broken engagement, she sensed. The clerk still wore her ring, a small diamond sparkled in the band. "It is not for me."

"Ah, for your man then," the words weary and sad. She dropped the duster and opened the gate, removed the coat from its mannequin. "He must be large, your man," she said, holding out the coat.

She only nodded. "The price," she asked. "Will this do?" She put the change from the gold coin on the counter.

"It is a fair exchange," the clerk said. "He is a lucky man."

And she left with the coat draped over her arm, indeed a heavy and handsome coat. A lucky man. He would be pleased.

She headed for the flat where he lived with his ill wife. She knew the address on If Street although she had never entered. She knew the rules. He could not leave her, his wife, because she was ill and they lacked money for medicine. He had come to her when she worked as a seamstress in a small shop on the waterfront, bringing with him yardage of taffeta, to fashion his wife a dress. Piecework. With each stitch she learned his wife's form, with each stay, her small waist, her bodice. But she had never seen her face.

She had had a room then above the shop. Her mistress was kind. And he had come to her there after she had finished the dress, desperate with longing. He must have her. He would have her. His ardor was deep, plain. As proof of it, he brought her the small gold band for her pinkie, the fine cashmere shawl. But she said, No. It was wrong. His wife, sickly. And when he had at last accepted her resolve, only then did she give herself to him, only then to find that she had given herself so totally that no part remained to herself.

Often, she had watched the window of his flat at night, hoping just for a glimpse of him moving across the yellow square of light. But she did not violate his interdiction. She did not knock on the door. She was content to receive him in her room, to love him, to buy him small treats: marzipan, and tangerines, hazelnuts which she cracked for him with her teeth picking out the meats with her sewing needles, a pair of kid gloves, a leather satchel. Gifts small enough that he could explain them.

But this was before her mistress had died. She had found no other situation and lived at the edge of life now, hoping only for a glimpse of him. He could not help her, she knew. He worked as a chandler, and his wage was small, barely enough to keep his wife in palliatives. Laudanum was dear, but it eased her, he said, eased her pain. His pain. She respected pain, so she had respected his adjuration that she not seek him at home.

And she had not. But this was different. The coat. She would only rap on his door, whisper, hand him the lovely coat while his wife kept to her sickbed. Then she would leave and be glad because she had seen him, seen him again if only for an instant, a whispered exchange in a hall. She had not seen him in weeks. Yes, that was what she would do.

And so, she found herself on If Street, at his building, in its foyer, up its steep flight of stairs, to his stout wooden door with his name on the brass plate, *Gregory Dorset*, her knuckled fist wrapped around the two remaining coins and rapped softly until the door swung to and she beheld the face which had rested next to hers. That face. Those brown eyes, soft and warm as mud. That pouty mouth.

"I told you not to come here," he said. His head snapped, checking the hall.

She extended the coat, seeing aspects of the room behind him, surprised by the warmth which seeped from it (coal?), the sumptuous red of the walls, a marble stand with a vase of peacock feathers, a damask settee. He drew himself larger as if to prevent her view. "Go," he said. "I will find you later."

But then she appeared over his shoulder, his pretty wife. She knew his wife by her diminutive torso. She knew the dress which she had stitched, the slippery stiffness of the taffeta as it rustled beneath her fingers, the color of Corncockle, as iridescent as a starling's wing.

"Who is it?" she asked, peering over her husband's shoulder. Her voice tinkled like tiny bells. She saw her sole pain, her childlessness, and her puzzlement when she failed to recognize this urchin at her door.

And her husband answered without once removing his

darkling eyes from her face, "It is the seamstress whom I had stitch your dress. She's come with a coat which I asked her to mend." And he took the coat and closed the door.

And she knew. She knew that the wife was not ill. She knew that there was no laudanum, no want. She knew that he did not love her. She knew that their afternoons together were tawdry, paltry things, rags not worth the mending. And she realized with a start, that he, he alone, suffered no hidden pain, and she knew why. He had no conscience.

She had confided to him that their love had brought her pain, but that it was bearable, bearable because she would prefer to bear the pain for both of them rather than think of him feeling even a twinge. She could not bear it.

The coins clinked in her palm. She felt them growing heavier as she descended the stairs, sadness seeping under the doors, down the long hallways smelling of spices and ladies' perfumes unable to mask the secret aroma of death and betrayal, sickness, poverty, perversity, brutality all alchemizing into the coins in her palm. She could not bear it.

When she returned to the streets, she walked blindly toward the pawnshop. Even with her eyes lowered, she could feel the ghostly woe of strangers welling against her, rising like a full tide to engulf her. She thought she might drown before reaching him, so she quickened her step, jostling the crowds as she hastened, head lowered.

This time she did not wait; she opened the Dutch door without knocking, and the pawnbroker greeted her from behind his grate. "Back to the rag and bone shop, I see. Most come back."

Behind him she saw the consumptive woman shimmer, savagely beautiful. She saw, too, his new acquisitions. A wall of clocks: cuckoo, and pendulum, banjo clocks, moon-faced clocks, clocks with Roman numerals and clocks with none at all, all set at different times.

He followed her gaze. "Buying time," he said. He drummed his six fingers on the counter waiting. A clock gonged three, another nine.

And then she saw it. The room swam in fluttery light. She braced herself on a stool. The woman's head was cut, cut by the ax which had bobbed his fingers in self-punishment. He had murdered her, as ill as she was. He had murdered her in bed. He had not murdered the man who lay with her.

"I want my pain."

He chuckled his dry laugh. "Plenty of pain to go around, my dear. Seas of it." He extended his mutilated hands in a gesture of bounty.

"You did not tell me the truth," she said. "You did not explain the charm." The bodiless woman behind him mouthed a silent O and swayed just above him.

She set her coins on the counter. "I want it undone."

"And it shall be in part. But there are but two coins here. One is spent."

She nodded.

"On him?"

She nodded again and said, "And bread. Cinnamon." She tasted now what she could not taste earlier, the tang of cinnamon, the sweet exhalation of yeast and honey. The clocks ticked. A pendulum stopped swinging.

"Small price for truth, I think." He picked a key off a nail and wound the stalled clock, his back toward her.

"Please," she said. "I cannot bear it. It is too much."

"There is a condition," he said. The woman above him parted her persimmon red lips.

"Yes, there is always a condition."

"The pain which you have borne you will now be able to

inflict with no more than a stare. All the pain which you have accumulated, and stowed, and suffered in private, all of it will be distilled into your glance. You have but to will it and it will muster in your eyes and strike whomever you behold. At your will, you understand."

"I understand," she said, "and I accept."

And the woman above the pawnbroker shuddered, then began to fade until she disappeared into the shadows cast by the flickering lights or became them.

She left the coins and picked her way between the heaps of clothes and pails and boxes which littered the floor. She did not glance back.

As she closed the door, she saw a bonneted woman scurrying toward her, a clock swaddled in a blanket. She turned her eyes to the cobbles. Not for her, these stores.

She understood what the pawnbroker had handed to her, the choice which she now must make: whether or not to let him, the chandler, feel just for an instant the pure light of the pain which he had caused her. And pain that clean, it *would*, bring him to his knees. Could she? Could she let him endure it just for an instant?

What did he, could he know about living on If Street? If my wife dies? If I had enough money to procure her care and we could move together? Italy, I think. If I were a stronger man. If I did not have obligations. If I had met you earlier, in another life, as a different man. If you had money. If. If implied then. Then endlessly deferred is never. But if. If pulsed with hope. If only. If only. A world of contingencies. Clocks ticked. Liars licked their lips. She had lived in the land of "If" until, until... But until implied then and consequence. She had stitched for herself time's foolish motley while he had incompleted sentences and left her dangling there, an elliptical fish, between sea and boat, needle and thread. A fish fool, creeled and crueled. She had no consequence. But if. If...

And then. For the second time but with her hand coinless and lighter now, she clutched her shawl about her and walked If Street, entered his foyer, climbed his flights, smelled the perfumes and spices but no longer the cloying sadness lingering in his halls and reached the door with the brass plate. *Gregory Dorset*. Door set. Set against the world without to ensure the world within of coal heat and peacock flourishes and flourishing wives and handsome wallpaper. And brass. Brass. Test metal, mettle.

And then she paused there waiting with all the painstaking love that she'd stitched into a gown poised in her hand, absently rubbing thumb against the base of her pinkie, waiting for her empty fist to knock, knock senseless those brown, brown eyes, time ticking in her heart like a clock with no hands. A decision snapping like a thread. A seamstress' riddle. If Street.

# TENEBRAE

"The phone is always ringing. How can anyone sleep around here?" Mrs. Summers who wears her hands like earmuffs, shouts, "It's 7 o'clock in the morning."

Mrs. Summers' son, who has just hung up the phone, says, "OF course no one can sleep. There's a ten-ton truck dumping twenty tons of railroad ties onto the front lawn. It's digging up the yard. Look at the tires on that monster. It's going to kill the grass."

"I told him not to order that wood. He's too old for this kind of work. It's 104° out. What's he trying to prove? He's got a plastic hip, a bad leg. What's he trying to prove?" Mrs. Summers' hands, useless, feather-flutter like emu wings as she asks, "I can't stop him, can I? He's a grown man, a *stupid* grown man."

For the first time since his parents' arrival, Mrs. Summers' son agrees with her. "I told him the deck's fine the way it is. I told him I didn't care if a few of the steps were rotting."Mother and son stand side-by-side in the air-conditioned living room watching Mr. Summers limp out to the dumped timbers, which are twenty feet long. He carries a small reciprocating saw. For the next three hours in 104° sun, Mr. Summers proves his wife's hypothesis: the saw blade is too short and the saw too weak to cut through a creosoted railroad tie. After three hours, Mr. Summers is soaked and exhausted. The timber is sawn one-third of the way through. The saw has no teeth and is now a reciprocating butter knife.

Mr. Summer enters the house and dials U-Rent-All to lease a chain saw. Mrs. Summers dials the lumber yard to come and pick up the remaining unsawn ties. For $20, Mr. Summers leases the buzz-saw for the day, cuts the tie into thirds, digs up the old, rotted deck steps, and embeds the new ones. At intervals, Mr. and Mrs. Summers scream at each other.

Their son, whom they are visiting, loads his daughter and puppy into the car and spends the day on the beach. When he returns from the beach, Mr. Summers is channel-surfing; Mrs. Summers is jabbing toothpicks into cubes of Velveeta on a blue Fiestaware plate. She offers her son one as he passes through the kitchen.

"I've eaten," he says. He puts his daughter to bed, reads "The Three Little Pigs" to her, and watches her fall asleep as he does on visitation days, Mondays, Wednesdays, and alternate weekends. He is divorced. While his daughter's cheek, smashed into the pillowcase, rouges feverish with sleep, he strokes her hair, worries about wolves who huff and puff little houses down. Then he exits quietly, leaving the door ajar, and goes to the living room to watch his father watch TV.

His father drinks bourbon. His mother passes cheese cubes. Roseanne Connor screams at Dan Connor in her tinny TV voice and yanks her hair out in brown mock-mad horns. His mother talks to him about the great buy she got on yellow two-ply paper towels. Of course, they're not the brand you usually buy, and they're not blue, but they're two-ply, and three for a dollar. Blue and red lights from the television irradiate Mrs. Summers.

Mr. Summers pours another bourbon. Mrs. Summers tells him he's going to kill himself. Mr. Summers slides the patio door aside to go out for a smoke. Mrs. Summers says he's going to kill himself, then advises her son on where to site the umbrella clothesline. Near the back door, so he won't have to walk too far.

"No," her son says, "I don't want it there. I'll be tripping over it, and it's an eyesore. Besides, I want to put up a run for the dog there."

Mrs. Summers reminds her son that she warned him not to get a dog.

Mr. Summers slides back in the patio door and gets another bourbon and warning from his wife that he's killing himself. Mr. Summers, who is very tired from the sawing and digging in the 104° heat and just wants to relax, prompts several more warnings from his wife before the phone rings and Mrs. Summers complains about the phone's incessant ringing. "It's ten PM," she says. Mrs. Summers is expert at reading thermometers and clocks.

At ten PM, I am the person calling as I was at seven AM. Mrs. Summers' son, Gordon, my boyfriend, answers the phone. "It's been a rough day," he says. "It's going to be a long week." And he relates the incidents of the day as I've recounted them. I haven't met Gordon's parents, so I murmur sympathetically as Gordon says, "and then" and "can you believe" and "so I said." Generally, a character-based story has more life when you know the people.

Gordon's complaint about his parents grows tired of its whining. We plan my trip down there to visit the following week.

"Please tell your parents I'm sorry that I won't meet them this trip," I say.

"Poor them. Lucky you," Gordon says.

I'm uncomfortable when he says this. Later, I'll think it's a premonition. At the time, I only say, "You don't mean that."

After he hangs up, Gordon returns to the living room where his mother is passing cheese cubes and his father is passing out. Mrs. Summers, angry at Mr. Summers for being drunk, shakes him, screaming, "We come all the way up here to visit our son and you get drunk like you could any night at home." Mr. Summers opens one eye, then starts snoring loudly. Very loudly. Gordon suspects he's playing possum. Apparently, Mrs. Summers does also. With a whoop, she opens the liquor cabinet and empties the bottle of bourbon into the sink. "I'm not going to stand by while you kill yourself."

The possum rouses. "You're emptying my booze?"

"I'm emptying your booze."

"Give me that bottle."

"No, not that one or any of the others." Mrs. Summers holds a gin bottle behind her back. "What you going to do? You going to hit me? What you going to do with your son standing there staring at you?"

"Give me that bottle," he says. Mr. Summers bangs Mrs. into the counter as he wrestles the bottle away from her.

"You proud of yourself? Now what you going to do with that bottle?"

Mr. Summers stares at his son, the bottle, Mrs. Summers, his son, the bottle. "What, what am I going to do? I'll tell you what I'm going to do. I'm going to empty it down the sink." A man of his word, Mr. Summers empties the bottle down the sink. Mrs. Summers empties her bottle down the sink, saying, "And I'll help you."

"You'll help me; I'll help you." Mr. Summers up-ends a vodka bottle. Mrs. Summers tips a Canadian Club.

While they drain Gordon's liquor cabinet into the sink, bottle by bottle, he goes to bed and turns on the radio so he can't hear them. He gets up once to shut his daughter's door.

In the morning, Mr. Summers drives to the liquor store and charges $100 of hooch on his American Express to replace the contents of his son's liquor cabinet.

Of course, I do not hear these events until Gordon relates them to me at ten PM when I call the following night, and Mrs. Summers complains about the ringing phone.

These are the vignettes from the week of his parents' visit Gordon stores in his mental archives to relate to me on the first day of my visit:

**Monday**: Mrs. Summers says Snazzy, the pound puppy, is a pest because he drools, jumps, and pees on the floor.

"That's what puppies do," says Gordon.

Mrs. Summers reminds him that she advised him not to get a dog.

**Tuesday**: Mr. Summers mounts the garden hose bracket in the middle of the front of the house. In 102° heat, armed with a Philips head, Gordon mutters for an hour, removing the screws and moving the bracket to the side of the house. He trips on the hose and jabs himself in the stomach with the screwdriver.

**Wednesday**: Mr. Summers becomes the cham-PEEN hotdogger of the remote control. Hanging ten, he channel surfs the crests and troughs of the soaps. Gordon drives to the drugstore and buys foam earplugs, decibel rating: 26.

Mrs. Summers calls her granddaughter a brat because she riles up Snazzy, then complains because he's riled. Her grand-daughter throws a fit and a rawhide bone at her feet.

Gordon rents "Babette's Feast" at the Video Vault. His

mother keeps saying, "I don't get it." His father cracks the fresh bottle of bourbon, drains the level to the label, and goes to bed.

**Thursday**: While Gordon steams at the beach, his mother rearranges the living room furniture to improve the traffic flow. When he comes home, Gordon and Mr. Summers return the furniture to its original gridlock pattern.

Mrs. Summers stuffs a calzone and alphabetizes the spice rack.

**Friday**: Mr. Summers installs an oak toilet seat in the master bedroom bath, paints the dining room, and grouts the fireplace tiles.

Mrs. Summers hangs ivory vertical window treatments in the living room and bedroom. "Think of it as a house-warming gift," she says.

The family eats calzone stuffed with lo-cal cottage cheese. "I like it better with ricotta," Mr. Summer says.

"I'm not going to stand by while you kill yourself," Mrs. says and tsks about cigarettes, booze, high fat diets, high blood pressure, low blood sugar, and low energy while Mr. Summers drains the bourbon bottle incrementally in one of the highball glasses I ordered for Gordon as a house-warming gift.

**Saturday**:

A metaphor: I once camped cross-country with my family and watched the mud pots boil in Yellowstone National Park on an unusually hot July day. My older brother kept pinching my younger brother who cried which made my older brother feel successful enough to attempt Indian rope burns, noogies, and wedgies. My father, beset upon by a cigar-smoking Indian in fringed ultrasuede and full headdress, sagged in his pitch-smeared polo shirt and chinos, his face darkening like a bruise. The mud vat bubbled like pea porridge and smelled like rotten eggs. My mother bubbled with helpful suggestions about a nearby Holiday Inn and restorative powers of a hot shower and clean sheets. When Old Faithful blew, I understood the volatile, sulfurous forces beneath the surface that could contribute to such an eruption. After my father's blowout, we were all very quiet in the car driving to the Holiday Inn.

Gordon blows on Saturday when he comes home from the Super Stop 'n Shop with bagels and LITE cream cheese to find his mother dusting the living room furniture with his new face towel, a house-warming gift from Jerry, an interior designer who lives in the development. The towel, figured with frolicking bunnies, some merrily mating, has a matching finger-towel.

It isn't really the towel, or its newness. It could be a cigar-smoking Indian (who is really an Italian from New Jersey). It could be anything. Gordon fires, "What are you doing?"

"Dusting?"

"Why?"

"It's dusty."

"If it's dusty, I'll dust."

"I don't mind."

"I do. I don't want you dusting my house." Stress 'my'.

"I know it's your house. I'm just trying to help."

"Help? That's my brand-new towel. You don't dust with a towel; you dust with a rag. You want a rag, here's a rag." Gordon reaches into the cupboard under the sink, throws a rag at his mother.

"That's a nice way to say thank you for all we've done."

"Thank you? Thank you? Who asked you to do it? I didn't ask you to do it. I didn't ask either of you to do anything. What are you trying to prove?"

Gordon drives Mr. and Mrs. Summers to the airport. Mrs. Summers cries and says, "When you were a boy, I asked you what you wanted to be when you grew up, and you said, 'Happy.'"

"Yeah?" Gordon says, "I changed my mind."

Mrs. Summers, ignoring him, says, "I certainly hope you're happy now."

Gordon hugs his father and says, "Maybe you could visit in October. You could come out with me on poker night. We could have a few drinks."

"Sure, kill your father," Mrs. Summers says.

Gordon kisses his mother. He wants to apologize for the towel incident. He wants to tell both of his parents he loves them. But the setting is distracting -- all the travelers bustling around, all the travelers' bussing cheeks. All the luggage wheeling and reeling, the speakers crackling. Arrivals and departures.

"Have a safe trip," he says. Those are Gordon's last words to his father.

**Sunday:** Gordon meets me at the train. He's late, heavy traffic. In the car, he relates the week's incidents. As we commiserate about parents, how parents can't be anything but parents, the incidents become amusing anecdotes. But soon the tone will shift.

That first evening, Gordon takes me out to a crab house for dinner. We attend a "Temptations" concert with another couple. Gordon and I hold hands like teenagers in the backseat while Gordon rants about his parents' visit. The front-seat couple laughs, but then Gordon goes too far with an incomplete narrative about his father, a suspected affair with a neighbor's wife one year when his father was working nights and his mother was working days. And his father, stumble-drunk one morning, flushed the john and banged upstairs to bed. When Gordon entered the bathroom, he saw a squiggled condom floating slowly, circling on the surface of the bowl-water, trailing limp latex like a tentacle. He fished it out with a toilet brush and buried it in the backyard. He never mentioned the interment to either his father or his mother. But he wondered about the circumstantial evidence. After they moved out of Brooklyn, whenever his father or friends from the old neighborhood mentioned the couple who'd lived next door, Mrs. Summers said, "I hate those people."

The front-seat couple, "Ums." The husband coughs. The wife clumsily diverts our attention to a billboard of a bikini-ed swimmer, hawking beer.

Gordon squeezes my hand and says, "It's a mystery. I guess I'll never know what really happened."

I say, "I hope the Temps do 'My Girl.'"

The front-seat couple endorses the hope with enthusiasm.

After the concert, we have drinks at a mock-Jamaican bar, Seaductress. Gordon orders a tropical exotic, called "A Pain in the Neck" for the two of us. The front-seat couple drinks Lite beers. When we get home, Gordon gives me gifts: a vintage sarong patterned with Japanese lanterns, and an antique cutwork silk blouse. The sarong snug on the hips, sags on top. While Gordon smiles, he says, "That looks great," I wriggle out of it and slide back into my dress.

I kiss him, but I'm sad. "It's too much, Gordon. Dinner, movies, drinks, presents. It's too much."

"I just want to show you that I love you."

He shows too much, but I don't say that. I say, "Thank you."

Gordon undresses me. My sundress puddles on the blue carpeting. It's three AM. I know we will make love because we have not seen each other for a month. I know Gordon will take a very long time, that acrobatically he'll swing himself into different positions on, over, beneath my body. I know that he'll talk as he rubs me slowly, repeating my name to prove he knows I'm there, asking me what feels good, telling me what he wants to do next, that he'll take his time for my pleasure before, the hour being late, he'll drift into sleep before coming -- which is exactly what happens.

I lie staring at Gordon's insomniac ceiling. The air-conditioning rustles the new strippy vertical blinds which remind me of carwashes, of coming clean. Silently, I confess to the plasterboard my love for Gordon and my confusion about love, why it assumes the vocabulary of high school bio. lab. Why do we construct proofs of love as if it were only a hypothesis and not a conclusion? Why do we demonstrate it with all the wrong gifts as if deck stairs rose straight to the heart, as if sarongs wrapped up love -- a sure thing?

My teacher, Mrs. Knox, assigned us a dissection in bio. lab of a fetal pig. I wondered where all these unborn pigs came from. The mind's a dangerous tool; some things are intended to be unknown.

Ceiling, I've always concluded love is unknowable. Its unknowability makes it love. Ceiling, you or the therapist's office are the confessional of the fin de siècle 20th century, and I want to tell you this: I told a lie. I do not know for certain if I love this man who's fallen asleep cemented to me with dried sweat. On happier evenings, I swallow him; he drinks me. We transubstantiate ourselves with the exchange of bodily fluids. I've always concluded love . . . I fall asleep.

I wake to Gordon between my legs. We want to prove desire to each other. We want to erase the erasure of sleep. Unaware, Gordon nudges me to the bed's edge. My head dangles. The ceiling becomes a floor, rolled back for the dance. The floor becomes a furnished, gravity-defying ceiling. I gargle Gordon's name, the word in my throat, a trapezist, somersaulting through the air. "Gor-gor-don."

He gathers me in murmuring, "Poor baby."

It's a little scary working without a net.

We have breakfast on the deck. When I fetch the milk from

the refrigerator, the photos flutter, but the magnets hold the pictures; 19 of Gordon's daughter, Rebecca, 3 of Mr. and Mrs. Summers, 1 of me with my son Ryan in The Bubble Room on Captiva Island, my son who's home with his father, the man I'm divorcing for love unproved.

I like the Polaroid looks of Mr. Summers, a grinning broad face, a good-natured gut. During the week, I begin to revise the tone of Gordon's accounts of the parental vacation. I begin to sympathize with his parents and the facts. These are the facts:

Gordon and I bicker all week because I smoke cigarettes on the deck and leave the sliding door ajar, because sex turns sour on the fourth day, simply stops, the mattress snoring while I stare at the ceiling, because I express poorly my reservations about "The Crying Game" which he thinks is a perfect movie, because I drink too much at the neighborhood cocktail party and make an ill-advised remark about Levittowners which I don't remember in the morning.

Mrs. Summers overnight expresses a package to Gordon. The package contains three new towels folded lengthwise in thirds. I think it's a very classy way to say, "Screw you."

Because I like Mr. Summers' home improvements: the wooden toilet seat, the putty-colored walls in the dining room, the fresh grout, the deck stairs.

Because I step in a puddle of dog pee on Thursday morning as I search the refrigerator for seltzer. Because Snazzy chews my silk blazer, and drools on my forearm.

Because Rebecca teases Snazzy into a frenzy Wednesday night; the TV's blaring a Care Bears vid.; the stereo's blaring a Jonathon Richman CD. I keep stepping in dog drool while the carpenter's pounding, installing the new shelves in the dining room which I think is too dark anyway. I don't like ranch houses; they're too flat like the Eastern shore, and all of the area as far as I've seen is one vast housing development and strip of shopping plazas with interchangeable stores, and I don't mean to sound spoiled, but this isn't what I'm used to; I'm accustomed to living in a cape in a village in Connecticut where the air gets laundered daily by a northeaster or a sea breeze. And I'm trying to cook dinner in this prefab kitchen, in a wall-to-wall, wall-boarded imitation-wood-paneled house, envisioning that this will be my future.

The range hood fan rattles. Gordon doesn't own a whisk. The sauce is clotting; he doesn't own a strainer. The kitchen's not equipped; I'm not equipped to live like this. We eat a silent dinner on the deck. Snazzy's cold nose keeps snuffling my crotch. Rebecca's whining; she doesn't like the dinner, scallion-sauced shrimp. I miss my son Ryan; he'll eat anything. I miss my home. I panic quietly, I've got to get out of here. Privately, I alter my travel plans. I'll take the train a day earlier. I'll never come back. End of the line.

Washing dishes with the bunny-figured towel, I firm up my plans while Gordon reads to Rebecca. The carpenter lets himself out. The tape ends. The TV muses blankly. The refrigerator hums. I don't hear Gordon enter the kitchen, but hands wrap my waist. Lifting my hair, he mouths the back of my neck, he mumbles that he loves me, that he doesn't want me to go home. Home. Love. A foregone conclusion. I should hate him for turning the map of my life upside down, for turning me around and kissing me. My resolve dissolves.

But this story isn't about me; it's about Gordon's father, who dies two days after I return home on the train. When I step off the train in Connecticut, my relief is visceral. A gentleman in madras pants cinched with a whale belt carts my luggage for me. Home. It will be the end of us. I plan how I will tell Gordon I love him, but I cannot live south of the Mason-Dixon. I'll write him a letter, but that's too cowardly. I'll tell him on the phone.

Phones are about to start ringing. But first I have a dream, a dream about Gordon's father who will die the day after tomorrow and whom I've never met. Considering that we've never met and he's debuting in my subconscious, Mr. Summers is pretty casual about the introduction. He's grinning his Polaroid grin and carrying his prosthetic hip in his hands. He offers me a drink from the hollow of the hip. It tastes medicinal like gin. He says, I'm sorry I'm not here to take your call, but if you leave a message at the tone . . .

I say, "You called me."

Later this afternoon, I will think the dream a premonition, but this morning I only think it is anxiety about what I will say to Gordon when he calls.

When Gordon calls, he says, "I have bad news."

I'm relieved; I think he's going to initiate the breakup.

But he says, "My father's in the hospital. He's had a mild heart attack. They're going to keep him a few nights to run some tests."

My pre-recorded message rewinds. Instead of telling Gordon that we won't work out, I'm telling him I love him. I'm telling him his father's going to be okay. I'm telling him that I wish that I were with him. I'm telling him his father knows he loves him, that it's fortunate they've just had the visit. I'm thinking that some of these reassurances are lies, which ones, I don't know.

The deus ex machina for bad news is the answering machine. When Gordon comes home from the beach the following day, he gets it. He calls and tells my answering machine, "My mother was right; my father killed himself. He had a massive heart attack getting out of bed. I don't know what to do." I replay the tape several times and listen to Gordon cry. When I call Gordon, I get his answering machine. He's on a plane to his mother's. He leaves the number of a funeral parlor on the tape. When I call the number, I get an answering service. Voice mail. I say, "This message is for Mrs. Summers: Mrs. Summers, I'm sorry to intrude. I'm sorry I didn't get to meet Mister, Frank. I love Gordon, and I know how much Gordon loved his father, and . . ."

There the tape cuts me off. I'm not certain how I would have completed that ellipsis. Perhaps I would have said what I later think on the phone while I listen to Gordon:

That his pain is so intolerable to me, that I take it as my own, tolerate it and know I love him, that I'm sad because his father will be absent on the day of our wedding, that loving is like tackling a railroad tie with a reciprocating butter knife. It's so hard to get through, but we do. Persisting, we do. That we will miss love's doggedness, its waxy face towels, its sliding doors, its bad habits, empty bottles and spent cigarettes. It's a mystery, a small funeral in a backyard in Brooklyn. It's the details that wear you down; it's the overlook, the actions which, remote, we look beneath to find love in a cube of Velveeta, in an emptied bottle, or a railroad tie. It's the details we will miss. It's what we do not say. And I say none of this. While Gordon talks, I listen.

When I call on the morning of the funeral, I get the answering machine. It's shocking to hear the voice. "Hello, you've reached the home of Ilene and Frank. We can't come to the phone right now, but if you leave a message at the tone . . ." I hang up, shaking. I recognize his voice.

When Gordon calls later, he tells me about the funeral. He says his mother is holding up. She even made a joke about the money they'd save on cigarettes and booze. He's sad because his father will miss that visit in October. He's sad because he didn't tell his father he loved him that day at the airport. He's sad because the visit was so testy. He says, "I wish you were with me. I just need you naked, holding me." He says he thinks he should stay a couple weeks to be certain his mother is going to be okay. He says he's surprised by all the friends she has, the clubs she belongs to -- golf, pool, bridge. "I don't know what I thought their life was like," he says. "I thought it was shopping, eating, watching TV."

When Gordon stops talking, I ask, "Do you want me to fly down? I could come down for a few days anyway."

"Would you do that?"

I hesitate, just a pause like the empty space in a satellite call. "Yes."

"Why? You can't tolerate the heat. You hate to fly."

I don't answer.

Another metaphor: My mother taught me how to bake bread. Yeast is delicate. You mix it with warm water, sugar, a little salt, and wait until it bubbles. When it bubbles, you know the yeast is still alive, the bread will rise. Then you add the flour. It's called proofing. A chemical reaction to ensure the dough will rise. Gordon needs proof of love.

"Are you still there?" he asks.

Long distance, silence is costly.

"Gordon," I say, "I can't explain this, maybe it's the photograph, but I know I would have loved your father. I think we would have laughed together."

"When will you come?" Gordon asks.

"If it's okay with your mother, tomorrow."

I hate those little machines in airports which dispense insurance policies. They remind me I'm about to place my soul's trust in an aircraft body. But I'm going to meet Gordon and his mother, so I swallow hard, pass the machine, the security check, and I board. I check my purse for chewing gum, my return ticket. I watch the flight attendants, glorified waitresses of the sky, dispense pillows, demonstrate emergency procedures with their mannered skits. Their cosmetic composure doesn't fool me a bit. We steward ourselves. The rest we trust to luck, randomness and speed, the pilot's expertise. I fasten my safety belt, ready for take-off, revving to hurtle, ears popping, into the future as wide, as wild, as endless as sky. My heart in my throat, my soul cupped in my hands, I close my eyes. Departing, I imagine arriving, kissing Gordon in a strange, busy airport at the baggage carousel, tugging my wheeled, over-stuffed suitcase behind me which will irritate Gordon as it always does. We'll argue briefly about my over-packing. He'll insist on pulling the bag, complaining as he hauls it, proving love. Love, or the details of it.

# THE CORNER OF DREAMS

Remembering is not the negative of forgetting.
*Remembering is a form of forgetting.*
—Milan Kundera

They had separated years ago. At first, she remembered him, his endearing eccentricities, how he drank his coffee cold, his cola warm. For many years, October made her think of the thick worn leather of his brown boots, September of his body beside her in the car as they turned the wrong way down a one-way street. Certain light, the blue tilted light of the fall, made her remember his eyes behind his glasses while he lay in her bed on his stomach reading, eating pie. Then she forgot about the pie, about the street, about his boots and cold coffee. Like pages, the days ripped them from the book of her memory. They kited off, somersaulted down streets and alleys in cities which she had never visited, cities which had no names. She rarely thought of him now. But sometimes at night when the moon slid a silver sleigh rocker across the sky, she skidded into soft dizzying dreams of snow. Her bare hands before her, dazzled by the sifting puffs, she'd wander forward in a blizzard, her breath huffing a small path ahead of her.

Occasionally small cardinals darted red from the white eddies appearing like sudden gouts of blood, then dried to nothing before she could startle, flying like the moment before one can identify wonder. She felt as if she were falling horizontally through space and time. Her white dress froze in stiff pleats. Her hands marveled at the snow.

Then she found the red thread of the dream. Because the dream was snow, white every which way, she might have found the thread, or it might have found her. Had it waited for her on the ground or sailed into her hands from a magical sky? Regardless, she followed it or reeled in the scene which advanced; she could not be certain. But gradually the filament threaded to a red bed.

The red bed on the white hill tilted a sky, a paler white, the fragile ecru dome of an egg which wanted to be cracked. Approaching, she wound the thread around her hands until, by the time she reached the red bed, it bound her hands, cut her hands. Bleeding. He was there, he was there from long ago. He was lying naked on the bed, his eyes pooling with the blue light that was himself. But she could not hug him because she had no hands. Instead, she bent to kiss him, perched at the precipitous rim of his gaze, plunged in, her feet kissing the air goodbye with a splash. The red thread unfurled a pearl necklace of bubbles. When she resurfaced, her eyes were full of water, his hands were full of olives. His breath smelled like an almond tree, blossomed on her neck, her cheek. His tongue snailed into the Nautilus shell of her ear. His hands brushed her body with the sound a clock makes when it stops ticking. The world turned blue because she was staring at it with his eyes. He smiled. He said, "Home."

But perhaps the almond tree, which was now sprouting olives, said, "Home." She could not be certain of the source because she knew that she was there. Home, she said. But she felt something tugging her, yanking at the hem of her dress, trying to pull her under the bed. A window framed itself beside the bed. She stared through a mirror of crackled glass, feeling him behind her, feeling behind him, behind something, someone else. Her. She. The one he would not leave.

Always she awoke, like the snap of a wrist, like the rim of a bowl, like an egg cracking. She awoke to her ceiling which was trying to stare her down. Although she slept alone, the bed rumpled. Fear knotted around her waist like a sheet. She did not need to be reminded that she missed him. Regret, like time, like loss, was cruel.

She wanted a dream assassin, some hooded scythe-bearer to sickle her dream at the roots. But the Yellow Pages listed no dream-slayers, so she made, instead, an appointment with a Palm Reader.

The Palm Reader's kitchen smelled like cola and wax and dry skin scraped from feet. Her table was covered with oilcloth figured with clocks. Dirty, linty slippers sprouted wild and fuzzy on her feet. Wearily, a teapot sizzled on a red woodstove. Her duster was the shade of green that makes flies weep. Four stiff hairs bristled long from her chin. Her coiled gray hair was a skullcap of crossed bobby pins. The dreamer stared into the picture of Christ which the palmist had taped to her forehead. Gouts of blood streaked from His crown of sorrow. The palmist read between the lines.

"You want to kill this dream?" Her voice was the sound of sand shivering on paper.

The dreamer nodded.

"Some dreams are not meant to be awakened. You know this?"

Again, she nodded.

"You know about the butterfly dreaming he is a man dreaming he is a butterfly dreaming he is a man and so on and so on?"

The dreamer spoke. "I am dreaming my life in reverse; in reverse my life I am dreaming."The palmist grabbed her hand and slapped the palm open. She studied it as if she wanted to accuse it of something. "Aporia," she said.

"What?"

"Aporia. The pathless path. You are walking on a path that is not a path until you walk it, and it begins to fork and fork. One of the fork tines is stunted. Blunt. Your love line split once."

She squinted. "And ended. Love ended, but your life runs on long, a tired runner. You have lost someone."

The dreamer nodded. "But do you see someone?" she asked. "Someone else? Someone later?"

"I see," she said, "only a red bed."

At this, Christ wept blood. The tears spilled into the dreamer's open palm and ran through her lines, fibrillated into tinier and tinier tributaries. She remembered once telling her blue-eyed lover that his hands were small. "Small?" he had asked, incredulous and pressed his palms to hers.

"Large," she said, feeling the press of his hands, feeling her hands shrink into his. A palmer's kiss.

The worst violence was bloodless. A turned head. Virgin bed linen. The unscreamed scream. The letters composed in anger at midnight, never mailed. A retreating footstep. The echoes of snow falling.

When the dreamer raised her eyes, the stare of the palmist met her. "Do you want me to tell you what you already know?"

"Can you kill the dream?"

The palmist shook her head. The picture of Christ fluttered to the floor. "You could try not sleeping. But you will be tired." She sighed and turned toward the red stove, poked at the lazy fire until it licked at the charred wood with angry dog tongues, then rested the poker in the grate. She turned and planted her elbows on the oilcloth. "You are no longer young. You will die soon, one decade, two. You will not have to dream of him much longer."

"It is not the dreams so much as the waking," the dreamer said. "It's all the coming and going. The loss over and over again. I'd just like to burn the bridge between them."

The palmist patted her pinned hair. "The lines are the lines." Her words were calm, but her hands shuddered suddenly like miller moths as they responded to the lit scene which they had foreseen sketched in the palm: the dreamer rose. The dreamer's smile curled as bitter as browned rose petals. She paused and delivered these lines which sounded rehearsed: "The dream is the product of my life. My life is not the product of the dream."

She grabbed the hot poker from the grate and grinned with awful teeth as she wrapped the orange-red rod with her right hand. "Flesh." The teapot hissed.

"I am sorry," the palmist said later, cradling her blistered red claw. "I am sorry. I knew. But I could do nothing to stop it, stop you. There is no point in corking a bottle that is empty. What will be cannot be diverted. It is. Like dreams. Like love."

The dreamer laughed. "It is done," she said. She stared at her hand as she would at a wingless bird.

When the palmist kissed her goodbye, the four stiff hairs raised pinpricks of blood on the dreamer's cheek.

Before she went to bed, she bound her red hand with white gauze. She slid between white sheets. She felt at peace for the first time in many years, like a blank sheaf of paper neatly pleated in an envelope. Her hand throbbed, holding her from sleep for hours. Then like a drunk, sleep lurched in, stumbled, and fell heavily on her. The snow cooled her aching hand. Blindly, she swiped through the snow, snatching red birds. She snapped off their heads and drained them, dotting a path in the white world so that she could find her way home. Who would have thought them to have so little blood? She crunched their bones like twigs in her sore hand.

She found the red thread and snapped it. A red bed slid down the hill. Was it empty? Her heart threatened to batter its way out of the cage that was her chest. No, he, the blue-eyed sat on the bed.

He spoke first. "I do not know why I am here," he said.

"Who are you?" she asked.

He shook his head. "Who are you?"

She sat on the edge of the bed. The sky had the glossy whiteness of a scar, flesh with memory. She stared at the naked man beside her on the bed, remarking little about him except that he had no sex.

"I forget," he said. He smelled like burning flesh.

"This is worse. I think this is worse. I don't know. The pathless path. I forget." They sat for a long time. They forgot each other.

Across the street from the dreamer, the insomniac was pacing, considering brandy. Movement in the streetlight drew him to the window. His thoughts flitted, jittery like bats in and out of light when he, sudden, saw his neighbor emerge from shadow. She was naked. Her body was long and white and slim, a glimmer of memory, a sliver of moon, ciphered slim as a sheet of mica. He trembled at her beauty. She was walking through the rose bushes near the hemlock tree, atop which teetered a thumbnail moon. The rose branches snatched and snagged her, tangled her hair. But she kept walking through the night that was the color of the smell of grass in June at midnight. At first, he thought she was mad, then drunk. Then he saw her glazed eyes. He knew then that she was asleep, lost in the dream maze where every door is a window is a mirror is a door is a wall, where every line is a box within a box. He felt someone watching her, someone beside himself, watching her the way one watches a lover, naked, rise to part the curtains on a yellow morning, waiting because soon, any instant she will turn, she will turn just slightly so her face is glimpsed over her shoulder and smile. The world turned on such smiles. He knew she was being watched by someone in her dream. He knew she was mad and drunk and asleep and stupid in love and wound up in ribands of time. He knew these things because he had, over years of not sleeping, grooved a path in his pine floors near the windows. A palmist once told him with a shrug, "You could give up sleep." Small sacrifice.

He watched the winds ruffle, unfurling the white bandage from her hand, spin it into the thorns of the bushes, tangle round and round, giving darkness a shape. His nervous finger dialed the police.

"A sleepwalker, yes. No. Not stalker. Walker. I am afraid she will hurt herself."

The dreamer tugged on the bandage, following it around and around the brambly bush. He thought of the thorn-thatched skin. The tiny scratches etching with blood. Skin. A cut. A red line. She forever lost in the ribands of crossing time.

"Where is she? Here. Where? The address." He chuckled. "Here. The corner of East and Dreams."

# TATTOOS

Walter's in the hot tub. He says, "I was going to get another tattoo, Alan. Remember? But I bought that vase instead." (He pronounces it voz.)

While Carol watches, Alan smooches him sloppily. Smack and slaver on his bee sting lips.

Carol is sitting in the Adirondack chair next to the tub, lazily scratching her thighs with her striped nails, orange and black, Halloween colors. But it's the Fourth of July. Dusk. "I'm waiting to get a tattoo in Samoa." The condensation from her martini glass puddles miserably on the chair arm.

"Ooh," Walter says. "Samoa, and what part of the anatomy is that a euphemism for?"

Carol snickers. Walter used to describe it as a pony's snicker, more like a nicker, soft and thatchy. Like something you'd like to curl up in. She says, "I can't get a tattoo. Fear of pain. I get migraines."

Walter says, "Joan Didion wrote about migraines."

She says, "Joan Didion is a migraine"

"What's it like?" Alan asks, backing into a jet. His blonde hair is spiky and dark with moisture.

"I don't know. I've never been to Samoa."

"No, what's a migraine like?

"Like? Like? It isn't like anything. It's a migraine."

When Walter is drunk, he starts composing eulogies or elegies. Walter is drunk, so he is composing impromptu. "My mother," he says, raising his green-stemmed glass. "How to characterize my mother and the meaning of her life? She was a small fast woman who made you think of shades of green, especially that shade of instant pistachio pudding which rural ladies are so fond of converting into salads. She was decidedly not mixed greens. So, on this solemn occasion, I think that she was a small fast molded salad. An unmixed green. A definitively defined chemical dye green. And she was loved for her shade of green." He goes on.

Carol thinks that this is fun. Or something like it. At least it isn't her life, the rest of which is categorically un-fun. Okay, it isn't fun. But it's different. Like Texans. Texans were definitely different. From everything. Except Texans maybe. Everybody she knew from Texas had a name to rhyme with the state: Lex, Rex. Even Tex, exact rhyme. Why did they do that? If there was some nominal rhyming gene, pity the poor sap who was born in Idaho. Hi, I'm Lida-beau from Idaho. Or Alaska. Hello, I'm Raska from Alaska. "I dated a Rex once," she says. Then she lies; she doesn't know why. "Rex from Alaska. Isn't that funny?"

"It isn't funny at all," Walter says. Walter says everything as if it is the last word. Carol hates that about him, but he's usually right. The right last word. Bon mot juste.

"Now Rex from Vermont. That's funny. That's hilarious."

Alan is laughing so hard that he's nearly drowning himself.

Suffering sycophants, Carol thinks, but she keeps it to

herself. When Alan is flirting, he'll laugh at anything. Anything. A hydrant. A cancer riddled forensic cadaver. Carol wants to get laid. But she doesn't want to get laid *that* much, not enough to fawn. But really Rex from Vermont *is* funny. She chokes on her cigarette so that she won't have to laugh. Coughs. Admires her fingernails.

Everyone in Vermont is named Duncan, or Cameron. Earnest designer names. Except for the real people. They were named Gary or Carl. But they were a diminishing breed. She'd had them all -- the Duncans, Camerons, Garys, and Carls, after Walter left, after the migraines, the bad period, before Ohio.

There was always another man. Names. Men. Just never the right one. And when you couldn't remember their names in those sad bleary, chary, rumple-sheeted mornings, it didn't matter. They were still all Duncans and Garys and wanting coffee. Hell, doll, if you want coffee, hit the diner. What am I? Your waitress?

In the morning, you didn't just want to shower, you wanted to douche your sorry soul with disinfectant. Shlub-b-gon. Now there was a household spray that could make Wall Street become Ceiling Street. Better yet, Through the Ceiling. Street.

Alan says, "I've never had a migraine."

Carol thinks that only smart people have migraines -- smart and depressed people -- like Joan Didion, like herself. But she isn't like Joan Didion. She's not that smart, and her migraines don't make her successful. But she is more successfully migraine material than Alan.

Walter says, "Ohio is funny even if you're not from there which is not there of course. Thank you, Ms. Stein. Even when you don't try to rhyme it. Ohio is funny."

"Only from far away," Carol says. Carol lives in Ohio. A place where people don't try to rhyme except when they are trying to write poems, jingle-jangle doggerel pomes. Rhymes with gnomes. They think that pomes are poetry. Fiction is lies. Prose is prosy-prosaic and the way normal people talk and write. She is not normal enough to live in Ohio. Now Illinois. If she lived in Normal, Illinois, she might be normal enough, normal enough to live in Ohio. States of mind. States of body.

Life in Ohio. She hopes that it is a temporary disorder, a pimple on prom night, the prom night which is her life. Sort of. It lacks the hopefulness. But it has the inevitable conclusion, the randy grope in the borrowed car by a guy whose whole life is a pimple. Pimpledom. Kiss him? I'd rather kiss roadkill. And he's your date with destiny. Life in Ohio.

Most of life is killing time. And no death rattles. Living in Ohio is killing time. Killing her. She moved there when she still looked thirty-something. She is staring fifty in the death mask, and she can't get out of Ohio. In the mirror, she sees the lurking face which she will become, the pouched brows and cigarette furrows.

When she and Walter were separating, their counselor said that she was manic, he depressive. Together, they constituted a pathology. Calling Dr. Caligari. Send this one *into* the closet.

Alan is busy snorking himself blue. Walter is composing a eulogy to Ohio. "The place where people don't have to have personalities and are suspicious if you do, where post-dated pork rinds are one of the four major food groups and iceberg lettuce doth a salad make. The state where the cling peaches cling."

"Oh, stop it," Carol says. "It isn't like that." But it is, at least to chauvinistic Northeasterners.

Alan is snorting water out his nostrils. It makes him look statuesque. Some grim-faced water god.

"Snorkel, Alan?" Walter asks and sips his martini. Coolly. Coolly as he does everything -- even hot sex. Coolly.

Carol hates him. Which is complicated. Because she loves

him. But she hates him for being a fag drinking martinis. It's so, so faggish. It would be bearable if she loved him. Except that she does love him. Maybe it's the martini. The martinis. Or Walter's sleepy cock delightfully awash in the bubbling knowledge that everyone -- at least this present everyone, not Green Mountain man Rex -- wants him. These three. These confused sorry hot-tubbing, martini bobbing three. Himself, Alan, she, they all love him with the same confused fervor -- except that it's different like Texans, Alaskans, Ohioans. Hot, cold, bland. The bland leading the bland.

Carol says, trying but not succeeding at keeping the covers on her vexation which is thwarted longing which she knows, which they all know, "Migraines are. What? I don't know." Conversation seems better than letting the truth well up, make them all sorrowful.

Walter sucks the pimento from his olive. "Yes?"

He expects her to be witty. Diverting. Screw that. "Painful. They're painful."

"Talk about a firm grasp of the oblivious." He snickers. His snickers are not the sort that you want to delve into; they are dismissive, cruel. Perfect in their own way which isn't Carol's.

Carol's drunk. But she digs her heels in, or maybe her striped fingernails. "Migraines," she says.

Walter waggles his hand; he's bored. Enough about migraines, let's entertain me. A firefly winks over his head.

Before he swung Bi, when he and Carol were still an item, they lived in Vermont. Walter hated Vermont. Way too wholesome. Too much nature. Too many peasant skirts and baby papooses. He wanted to live in a pretty place, but ritzier, a little more connected with the mainstream. Less Hippie Doodle Dandy. It was the mice that finally decided them. That fall in the farmhouse, they caught eighty-three mice. The Micecapades, Walter called that time in their life together. But it wasn't only the mice. The coyotes, too, and the gargling turkeys at night spooked Walter who was Irish and had a bad case of the banshees, inherited, he said from his mother's side. The McMurphy's. The coy dogs and turkeys sounded to him like banshees, and he'd be convinced that the sidhe had come for him and her, for him or her. It didn't really matter for whom they'd come; they had come. It was unsettling. Unsettling even after Carol had reassured him, as she'd reassure her son, palm on cheek or brow, that it was the coyote, or the turkeys, or the wind. Too much nature whatever it was.

So, they'd moved to the coast. Near Ogunquit. Better restaurants. Fewer peasant skirts. Lots more bathing thongs. On a gay beach, Walter realized that he loved Carol, but he didn't completely love Carol. He was incomplete.

He said that their love was theoretical, their relationship, highly theoretical. He dumped Carol. The pain was not theoretical. Enter Alan whom Carol found insipid. Exit Carol, following a job to Ohio.

Ohio. Land of the corn dog. Home of the drive-through grocery.

Alan is splashing and giggling. "Do you remember that Irish fag who kept singing *Whisky in the Straw* at the piano bar?" he asks Walter.

Carol knows that Alan is trying to close her out; he alludes to their gay contacts when he wants to exclude her. Walter's *new* life.

"It's *Turkey in the Straw*," Walter says.

"*Whisky in the Jar*," Carol, his *old* life, says and sips her martini.

"What's *Turkey in the Jar*?" Alan asks, no longer splashing.

"An Irish Thanksgiving," Walter says.

Alan hoots. Walter watches his antics, pleased but not betraying it. Walter is all about maintaining, maintaining calm, composure, former lovers. Not high maintenance, not low maintenance, just maintenance.

Carol admires her fingernails. "I wonder where they'll end up, she says. "My fingernails. Probably in a landfill somewhere. Einstein's brain rested for a while in an apple cider box, jarred, behind a beer cooler in Dr. Thomas' office. Lawrence, Kansas. Talk about being stuck. Antie Em, Antie Em. And Edison's last breath ended up in a test tube in the Ford Museum. I wonder where we'll end up?"

Walter swirls his drink. "In a sperm bank? Earning interest."

Alan titters, he slurps his martini. He isn't supposed to drink. Liver problems, a bout with hepatitis. She thinks about saying something, but, hell, it's not her liver. She's not her brother's keeper, not her former lover's current lover's liver keeper. She's feeling claustrophobic; she wishes that they could go somewhere but they are all too drunk to drive. Her own thoughts crib her. Claustrophobic memory, claustrophobic desire. Truth is, Ohio was not culpable. She was homesick everywhere and stuck in the boonies of her own past.

Every morning when she wakes up, she thinks of Walter with a blue-tinged tenderness, then a flashing stab of love. She doesn't want to think about him, but she does. She wishes that they'd worked out. She wishes that she could forget him. But she can't; she loves him. Still wishes. If wishes were horses, then the world would be overpopulated by horses. Wild horses.

Once, to escape Vermont, they took a vacation to Assateague. Walter loved the ocean; that's when he told her that he wanted to move to the coast. Bad move. Rewind that tape. Rewind. Rewind. But it's too late. Skip. Skip. Fast forward. Skip to the lou, my darling. *I'll find another one prettier than you.*

"I'd rather have another baby than another migraine," Carol says.

"How *is* your son?" Walter asks.

Enough with the migraines. Carol knows why Walter doesn't want to talk about migraines. Maybe a pinch, a dab of remorse, guilt. "He's grown and flown the nest, the coop. He's a Blue Angel."

"Aren't we flip," Walter says, then flops over onto his stomach.

Alan squeezes his butt. "You are so buff."

Walter groans. Carol wants to throw her blue-stemmed martini glass at him. But she hates breakage. Bricolage is more her style, all the odds and ends of her past, the oddments of love with which she cannot bear to part. Egad, she was a walking rummage sale.

After making love to her, Walter rolled over or stared at her down his nose, aloof, separate. She knew then that he no longer wanted her. Was remoteness love? Is that what kept him in her heart, her life. She could be on an Un-wanted poster, the Un-wanted poster child. White elephant. She is martini-woozy and sick of the whole shebang, this clutch of memories which was her life, this clutter of wants cramming the closets. Small wonder she couldn't get out of Ohio, her own private Ohio. It would take a fleet of vans to move all the stuff of her regret, vain hopes.

"Remember, Walter, that time I had the migraine." She is being cruel and relishing it. She is excluding Alan and loving that, too. The *old* life.

"Which time?" But he knows.

Alan slides out of the hot tub and grabs the pitcher, sloshes more into their glasses. Walter's looks precarious, perched on the lip of the hot tub.

"That time when I got the migraine and you drove me to the hospital."

He doesn't say anything, just reaches out and sips awkwardly at his martini, still adrift on his stomach, the water bubbling around him.

Boil, bubble, toil, and trouble. A witch's brew for certain. "See, Alan," Carol says, "when Walter and I were separating, I started getting migraines. One so bad that I was banging my head against the brick wall in our ever so tastefully appointed living room because it hurt less than the migraine, reminded me that pain knew quantity, quality. Some pain is nearly unbearable. But some is bearable."

"Enough, Carol," Walter says.

Last word. But she goes on. "No, Walter, it's not enough. So, Walter drives me to the hospital. My son Kelly was living with his father then. So, Walter drives me, and they want to do a cat scan because they think it might be an aneurysm or a brain tumor. And I'm hoping that it is. Some final cessation of pain. But it's only a migraine, and all I can do is manage the pain, all reflex, all animal, just managing the pain. And in the midst of this, Walter says, 'I can't handle this.' And he leaves me. Just leaves me at the hospital. And when I got home finally by taxi, I knew from the feel of the doorknob in my hand that he was gone. He'd moved out. The living room look deranged. Gaps where Walter's stuff had been. I ate Imitrex for days. Migraines make you very weak. It's all that management. Of the pain, I mean."

Walter has turned over; Carol can sense it. But she won't look at him. She stares at the red eye of her olive.

Alan freezes as if he's a kid playing flashlight tag or statues. The pitcher still in his hands. He sets it down and he gently frees Carol's hand from her glass and presses it. His hand is cold from the icy pitcher. His groin is level with her face, so she tries to train her eyes on the olive. He says, "That was a long time ago."

She can't see his abdomen anyway, because she is crying. Alcohol always makes her cry. She doesn't say anything because it *was* a long time ago. But last night was not a long time ago. Alan doesn't know anything about last night.

"There's no need for this, Carol. Walter and I both love you."

Sympathy, like alcohol, always makes her cry. She cries harder. She hears Walter roll back over onto his stomach. *Walter and I both.* A couple. How nice it would be to be a couple. She feels bilious with jealousy and self-disgust, knowing that she repulses Walter, too. All that messy female emotion. But she can't stop crying in this slovenly, pathetic, slobbery, snotty, phlegmy, gross-out way -- although she wants to.

True to form, Walter says, "Knock it off."

It angers her enough that she stops crying. "But enough about me. Let's be gay. Let's dance and sing and be festive," she says deliberately, airily, feeling like some insipid escapee from Gatsby who really wasn't so great.

"Let's be gay?" Walter says. "Oh, that's lovely. Really lovely, Carol."

"Oh, Walter, I didn't mean . . ." But she can't finish. She's too drunk to chase down the point, and who knows one's intent really. Whoever knows? And Alan is still clammily holding her hand, and she'd like it back. She really would. She feels smarmy, like a mendicant for pity, a supplicant for love. She cannot bear the posture. Prie dieux. Her psychic knees are bruised. "Let go of me," she snaps.

"Carol," Walter says levelly, "you are really over the top."

She feels more down at the bottom. No wonder he left her. She'd leave herself if she could. Ohio. Oh-why-oh?

"Tableau vivant," she says. "So it goes."

"So it went," Walter says.

She hates him again. But she apologizes. "I'm sorry," she says. She has revealed herself. She wants to reveal something else; she wants to tell Alan that she and Walter slept together last night. But she doesn't although she can feel it dangerously close, this desire to confess, reveal, breathing down her neck. Deliciously tempting. But it would be troublemaking, cauldron-stirring, to tell. No good could come of it. But still. That's what made consciousness so claustrophobic, that finally we have to endure our pains privately, and it made the claustrophobia of selfhood combustible. All the irrecoverable actions, the mistakes, and missteps. Shush, hush. Don't make a scene. At forty, one learns the value of repression -- all that sixties' confessional freedom was balderdash. Honesty wielded like a sledgehammer. Breakage.

Maintain. Retain. Contain. The bricolage of life at middle age. Private, private, private despite all the rummaging by strangers and former lovers and current ones. Self, self, self. Not ego just a surfeit of self and thwarted affection. This crumpled Rumplestiltskin of frustrated love. "Shoot," she says. "I'm miserable."

"We know, dear. We're experts on that front. You *are* miserable."

She hates how he inflects the sentence, but she really can't argue with it. And she feels Walter's alertness as if they were one animal, sensing danger. A deer's flicker of white tail, a bristle of forearm hairs transmitting telepathically from him to her. He is worried that she is going to tell. She settles smugly back into her chair. How lovely for once to have a full house in hand. Let him squirm. Let him bluff. Let him poker-face.

Alan slides back into the tub, nudging Walter aside. "I, for one, do not like being included in Walter's imperial *we*, Carol. I don't find you miserable at all."

"Why, thank you, Alan." He really is a nice man. Too bad. She finds it easier to dislike him when she can buttonhole him: inane. She thinks that he might be better than Walter deserves.

"Sorry," she says again. She's on an apology binge. Sorry, sorry, sorry for this sorry self in the sorry state of Ohio-mind whom I keep imposing on the universe until the final whimper. "Sorry. I'm sharp-tongued but essentially feckless."

"I'd say you're quite feck-ful actually, extremely feck-ful, hopelessly, distinguishedly feck-ful," Walter says which makes them all giggle. It's a relief.

Alan pats the water, splashing. "Come on in, Carol. It's relaxing."

"No," she says. "I hate to be hot." It would not be relaxing. It would be the opposite of relaxing. All that mixing of bodies, a bubbling broth of skins and sins. "No, but thanks."

She doesn't need a tattoo in Samoa, she doesn't need a tattoo in Ohio. She is already indelibly dyed, Walter needle-inked into her skin. No, she'd rather not mix it up with the boys. They are sitting side by side now, and Alan's arm is draped over Walter's shoulder. The casualness of the pose makes her gasp. She closes her eyes, but she still sees, sees herself and Walter in bed. On the floor actually. All those ridiculous poses, the contortions of love. Unlike Alan, she hadn't needed to laugh at Walter's wit. She didn't need to laugh at all. In gin-fueled lust, they'd hit the floor. Things went downhill from there. They spent hours rutting like bumptious puppies, enthusiastic if inept. Getting nowhere. Walter hadn't been with a woman for years, not since her. Sixteen years. He could get it up, keep it up, but he couldn't come. She'd just felt progressively stupider as the night and the floor wore on. Rug burns. Sore knees.

Truth was she always felt stupid with men. She didn't understand how the damn thing worked. She made a valiant try always, but she'd secretly thought for years that homosexuality made good sense -- aside from the whole procreation, be fruitful and multiply, dominion thing. A guy would know how to do it, what felt good, how the damn thing worked. If she were a guy, she'd probably seek one out herself. Why not consult a specialist. You wouldn't go to a backhoe operator if you had a cuckoo clock to repair.

Women habituated to not coming. They entered the arena with low expectations: a tussle, some tongue, a goose bump or two. She hadn't been thinking about herself, but she was sad that she couldn't do it for him. Couldn't get him off. It was probably strange to be with a bumbling broad after the years of expert men. She just was a little hurt, a little sad that she could no longer please him. Had she ever? And what was truly sad after all the gymnastics was this: buried under dumb lust was the keen brightness that she'd really wanted to offer him, this distilled and complete love. They could have simply held each other for the night. Nothing would have gone awry then. But they hadn't. Now in her nostalgia for Walter which she would lug back to Ohio, she would have this additional private pain: she could not please him. She could not even give him that. Mice-capades, the crumbs after the feasters have gone home to slumber off their indulgence. Not even that. All swept away.

Walter asks her, "Are you sleeping?"

"Brother John, Brother John," Alan chimes.

"No," she says. "I'm too tired to sleep."

When she opens her eyes, Alan is kissing Walter who accepts the kisses rigidly but tolerantly, holding his head like something fine, a Ming vase (voz). Dynastic aloofness his forte. Hold yourself apart, and you become fine, desirable. But breakable.

Pretty to look at. Pretty to hold. But if you should break it . .
.

She wants to tell Alan, not to wound him but to warn him.
He cannot love. This man, this Walter, his heart crowds with
self-love. And he does not care who gets lost in the crowd.
Morning bells are ringing. Din, dan, don.

Walter is now improvising for Carol. "Let us raise our
glasses to the dear departed Carol, Carol who had so much love
in her that she had to start spreading it around -- like manure.
For all the seeds to sprout. Carol of the long white hands, a
gardener's hands, Carol of the long white body and the long red
hair. Carol who dark-eyed nodded like one of her own sunflowers. Vermont garden variety. Carol withering into Ohioan
menopause without a pause."

"Stop it, please. Just stop it," Carol says. She covers her
ears. "It isn't funny." Walter: omega man. The last word.

"He doesn't mean it," Alan says.

She uncovers her ears and says, "How do you know what
he means?"

Alan's face contorts strangely like a strip of lime pith
knotted in a glass. Dregs. He says nothing.

Carol stares at the hands in her lap.

With a whoosh of water, Walter stands up. Shedding
sheets and beads of water. He really is beautiful. The moonlight tracing his musculature. His pillared thighs which the
tattoo encircles like a Greek frieze. Standing over them, he
looks unusually tall, larger than he is, larger than life, some
mortuary statue. Grand and grandiose. "I'm going in," he
announces.

Just like Walter. I'm going in, so the party moves except
that she doesn't and neither does Alan. Walter wraps himself in
a towel and disappears through the sliding glass door. She and
Alan sit in the frothy silence. Alan's head is leaned back on the

lip so she can only see his chin and hear the bubbles. After a while he says straight up into the night, the stars, the moon, the occasional litter of fireworks somewhere far away, "He's positive."

"I know," Carol says. "That's Walter. Always positive about everything, every whim or opinion he holds. It can be maddening."

"No," Alan says very slowly, raising his head until his eyes meet hers with a look which only later on rewind, replay, she will decipher as a look of profound pity for her, too profound even for the disgust which he must have felt. "No," he repeats. "He's positive. Positive as in HIV."

Carol has the whirlies, not from the martini, from this sudden centrifugal tumult of feelings, why's answered so fast that she can't take them in, but she can only think to ask, "You?"

He shakes his head. "Not yet. We're careful."

Careful. She spins. She *is* miserable. Why the invitation. Careful. Why the tumble on the floor. Careful. Why the . . . But, careful, don't go there; don't even think of going there. And if. And. And. There's nowhere left to go. Ohio is too good a place for her. A free state.

On Kelly's last visit, they drove through Appalachia, just driving around, desperate for something to do. They drove through the tiny town of Mineral, a smattering of tumble-down houses, sprouting like weeds along a curving road. The yellow-green creek water looked toxic. The overflow of poverty laying out its detritus on the scabby, patchy lawns. She drove through twice, the narrow valley dark, the vines tangling over this town, wondering how people stayed there, why they lived there. What vines kept them there, strangled them. She'd been unable to suppress the appalled awe in her voice when she asked her son, "How would you have liked to grow up there?"

"It's here, Mom," he said. "You've missed the point."

Alan is silent, but he still stares at her. She's out of small talk; all talk is suddenly small talk. A jarred brain. Din, dan, don.

Only the sound of bubbles breaking. Rewind. Rewind. And the sound of Alan silently sitting. The sound of an awful stare. His eyes hooded. And then she pauses, and she wonders for a second; has he told her the truth? His eyes curtained. A grin carves into his face. The silence between them beats a tattoo: Be careful. Be careful.

It's *here*. Please someone take care of us all.

# THE UNNAMING

*The limits of my language are the limits of my world.*
*—Wittgenstein*

A nd they were not ashamed, the man and his wife, naked and one flesh, still uncleaved and uncleaved. No Cain, no Abel, the unbegotten. And the woman (unnamed flesh of his flesh, the flesh named Adam), returned bone to bone, gave him a ribbing, he now Mada, he now sleeping, he no longer in need of helpmeet. So, she stood while he slumbered, he ribbed and comatose, and she, who forward or backward was Eve, palindromic, began the unnaming.

She unnamed the lion and the hyena. She unnamed the camel and the marmoset. She unnamed the chipmunk and the ocelot and the gorilla and the gnu. She just kept right at it. She kept right on unnaming long after most helpmeets would have called it a day. She unnamed with vim, until you'd think that she couldn't unname anymore. But she did. She unnamed every single beast of the field.

But she was not done. She unnamed every fowl of the air, plucking *kiwi* from the kiwi and *emu* from the emu and *dodo* from the dodo. She unnamed the blue-footed booby, the rufous-sided towhee, the yellow-bellied sapsucker, the coot, and the common loon. Unnaming the grackle was a delicate matter, demanding time and concentration, but unname it she did. She unnamed them all, and every living creature that she unnamed that was the unname thereof.

But she wasn't done. No siree, Bob, not by a long shot. She left Mada no helpmeet. She left him alone entirely. And death, she undid. And the root of the tree of knowledge, she withered, and with it the old duality of good and evil. And of every tree in the garden that she unnamed, the quince and weeping cherry and the blackthorn and coconut palm, she did not eat.

And out of the hewn tree of knowledge she built a raft. And she rode the waters, the Euphrates, Hiddekel, Gihon, and Pison westward out of Eden. Eve suffocated the dust and invented rain. She shriveled the plants and the herb of the field and execrated the seventh day and undid the heavens and the earth.

Until she saw Him in her own likeness.

Until she got to the beginning.

And in the beginning was the word.

And she undid it.

The last word was Eve's.

It was not logos.

She did not tell an unnamed soul what the last word was.

Last laugh.

AHA.

. . .

In the void, upon the formless earth, upon the face of the waters, unlit, undarkened, in the undivided days and nights, the unnamed drifted in a versing, endlessly reversing helical tide of time. A cow (who was not named cow) hovered above an unuttered green phrase. An unpronounced weeping cherry and flowering Judas wafted, dangling participles. There was a there there. There was still a there there. The there that was there was simply unnamed. It was not just a matter of perception, immanence. There was a vast vacuity, unlettered, unfettered by names, cut loose from meaning. A juddering silence uttered in all its a priori glory by shadowy presences who hung suspended beneath no names. Big bang-gangers in a swirl, a swerve, asymptomatic curling curves of time. Paraphernalia unparsed on parabolic time, awaiting names.

On what does the un-world, the ur-world rest? On the back of a turtle on four elephants on the back of a turtle on four elephants on the back of a turtle in infinite regress where the only sentence is an ellipsis, an unfinished curve into silence . . .

Eve who is herself, forward or backward, balances on the fulcrum. She is on the verge of a word. The Eve of Eve, the eave of Eve. She is the hinge of time. She is meaning, inchoate. She is an angel dancing on the pinhead of time, wingless wings aflutter. She is the vector opening up, a wedge, the vee, the cuneiform of semantic possibility.

Eve tilted.


Eve tilted to see what she would name them. She began with the flowering Judas and the weeping cherry, and she named them Eve and Eve. Then she turned to the grackle, and it, too, she named Eve. And the common loon, and the coot, and the yellow-bellied sapsucker, and the rufous-sided towhee and blue-footed booby, and dodo and emu and kiwi, all of these she called Eve. And the gnu, gorilla, ocelot, and chipmunk, these, too, she called Eve and that was the name thereof. Everywhere in every direction everything was Eve, an eponymous universe. Autotelic. Eve without end.

Eveveveveveveveveveveveveveveveveveveveveveveveveveve

Although she could no longer articulate it, Eve did not become the universe. In face, Eve disappeared. Eve dropped out, syncope, Ee, a silent scream radiating through electric muteness. There was no not-Eve, so Eve ceased to pertain which would have been the end of the whole shebang except that the universe got a big bang out of itself, and it exploded back into meaning.

Like stars, words reconstellated the universe, and Eve, herself again, began re-naming, first with herself. *Lilith*, she said. And she looked at all that was not Lilith, and it, too, she named but not with their former names, with new and beautiful names like qzhaimd, maodnfjgfndli, and widejup and kdsjffnc, and she saw what she had named and it was good. She named it all, filling the universal void with her ecstatic distinctions.

Except Adam, her old binary star, him alone she did not name. But she roused him regardless. And he set about the task of being unnamed. And in her renamed Eden she planted her garden. And in her new tongue, she said *Amen*. So be it.

# BABY I'LL BE HOME FOR HALLOWEEN

"**P**lease come home, baby, please. Annie, please." Imagines her shaking her head, her new sheep-cropped wool (*Take thee a barber's rasor*) where the pre-Raphaelite waves he loved used to flow as she says, "No, I'm nobody's baby. Have no home. No home on planet earth. No home in the universe. 'The high places shall be desolate'."

And desperate, he does what he always swears to himself he will not do after he slams the receiver into the cradle endlessly rocking: he screams, "That millennial clan, they're washing your brain, laundering your will, hanging you out to dry. They don't love you. Your lover doesn't love anybody but himself. I love you. No one will ever love you like I do."

Dead air before she says so prim he can hear the school marm mouth purse in the earpiece, "Arnie, I told you; he is not my lover. He is my sponsor."

"Sponsor? Sponsor this. That fucker is a fucker. If it fucks like a fucker, and fucks up heads like a fucker, then quack, quack, and fuck me, it's a fucker." His mouth is spit-screaming into the eye of the dial tone again and even before he hears the click, he's cursing himself, Damn you, Arnie, damn, damn, hot damn you. Slamming the phone into the cradle, talking himself down.

Whoa now. Gentle, son. Just hand it over slow and easy, pacing, cuddling the phone to his chest, setting it on the zebra skin hassock Annie left behind. *Thine abominations. Material possessions are immaterial.*

Trigger finger's itchy, wired to the redial, her new no-nonsense voice in his ear before the phone can ring, before it can even vibrate at the Millennial Compound.

"Arnold, admit that you are powerless. I refuse to enable you in your harangue."

Electronic silence hums like the wheels in his brain. There is a word, there is one word that will rewind the reel, recycle to the frame where it will all be right again, erase the last month, two months, bring Annie back home. One word, one word said in just the right tone, the tone of waking muzzily together, happy in spring on clean white sheets, muslin curtains stirring in the windows, daffodils trumpeting in the scraggly garden beds below the condo windowsill.

"Annie."

"My Twelve-stepper name is Warhead."

Dog turds in the daffodils. City spring. Car radios blaring migraine-shrieking loud.

Again. Try again. There is one tone, just the right tone that will summon Annie loving home. "Warhead," he says in a kiss-me voice, feeling like the stand-out lollipop in a Lilliput Land of all-day suckers. "Warhead, baby. I miss you. Come home."

The brain on over-drive, mouth in neutral, coaching himself: don't be desperate now. But the voice just can't make the team, can't keep the wheedle out of his tweeter, the woof-woof out of his woofer. "Annie-Warhead-sweetheart, come home for a minute, just an hour. Come for Halloween. You always loved Halloween. Your dress-up holiday where you can be anybody you want to be. Annie Warhead. Annie Warhol. Annie old anybody. Orphan Annie. Annie Oakley. Anne of Great Green Goddamn Gables. I don't care. Just come back, punkin. Give me a chance. I'll buy pumpkins like the old days. We'll scoop them out, carve each other's faces, be ourselves, like we were." Shut up; stop whining.

He can't; got a tremor in his tenor, a weasel tweezing his brain cells, a heart acupunctured with the red-hot rods of just-spent sparklers. "I'll buy face paints. We'll create each other. Go out for a drink, anywhere you say. Late as you want."

Her prissy voice so tight, his own mouth puckers sympathetically like a lemon with hemorrhoids, she says, "Arnie, snap out of it. Get a life. There's little enough of it left, Twelve-stepper Ezekiel prophesies."

"Goddamnit, Annie. Fuck twelve-goose-stepper Ezekiel. He's a has-been life insurance salesman with a Manson on the cross complex. You graduated summa-cum-gold mine tuition for Chrissakes. And now you're talking like Zeke's channeler."

But click. She doesn't hear "Zeke's channeler." Damn you, Arnie, damn you, he rants. You swore you wouldn't yell at her again. Finger transmitting neurons, starving street cur, begging love's pulse from the redial.

Rings once. Annie on the uptake in her limbo voice, "Twelve-stepper Omega advises me to tell you this phone call is at an end."

"Annie," he pleads, "just come home to pick up your things. I washed your silks, honey, that kimono we got in Hawaii. Remember, sweetie." Appeal to the past. "Remember how happy we were there on our prenuptial honeymoon."

Static scuffle on the phone, "This too will pass." Brother Omega's voice.

Lightning skitters up his spine, scintillates in his forearm hairs.

"Listen, Ace. I want to talk with Annie."

"Warhead has joined the group for evensong. Rest up. The world is coming to an end. 'Thou shalt burn with fire a third part. A third part thou shalt scatter in the wind.'"

"And the remaining third, Sport?"

"'Smite about it with a knife.' Have a nice evening." Dead zone dial tone.

Cheery group of Do-Bees, this Millennial Compound. Arnie watches his finger reflex-action the redial. Buzz-busy-buzz-busy-buzz-busy. Aw Annie. The phone catapults across the room, arcs, sinks into the faux leopard skin cushion of Annie's abandoned couch. Ugly couch, it stares at him with its thousand eyes. As the brother said, Arnie, rest up.

Arnie lies in bed trying to stare down his sleepless ceiling which stares back at him with the twin tiger heads of Annie's wrist tattoo, tattoo beating on him like signal drums. Holy Alpha and Omega, Batman, why in the name of the Almighty is Annie-knee-socks, Annie-Smithie mutilating her flesh for a Twelve-step Recovery Program for Doomsday Adventists?

He sweats into his winding sheet. Handled it all wrong. Why does love, why does loss make us do all the wrong things, make us do all the things, the very things that make loss the foregone conclusion? Should have shut up. Should have sent her flowers. Rosemary, that's for remembrance. Should have sent her a telegram: Can't STOP Stop loving you STOP Love is a door STOP Meet me at the bus STOP And the joint gets jumpin' when we do the Bristol STOP.

A twelve-step program for the end of the world? What's the point? When the googolplex fat lady sings, it's overeaters unanimous. The party's over. The world's consumed. Bought the fat farm. What we need is a twelve-step program for unrequited lovers.

I am powerless before my Annie-addiction. I'm on my bony twelve-bar-blue knees. "Baby, please come home. Baby, please come ho-o-ome. Baby, please come home down to Condo-town 'cause I love you so."

God grant me the serenity to reject that I cannot change the things I cannot change. Annie like a heartbeat, iamb in my chest, pulse in my wrist, Warhead. Annie. Warhead. Annie. Iamb yours. Too many stresses in a line. I'm tripping over my feet. "They flee from me that sometime did me seek."

Feel like Munch's radiating silent scream. Honest to Void, Annie, if will had hands, my arms would reach through the window, slink over the daffodil bed, snail-trail through the grid of streets, creep up the Compound stairs, drag you from Zeke's harem and rubber band you right back here into your rolling sweet baby's arms.

Phone trembles, jangles the small change on the night-stand. Rings right up the spinal ladder. Shit. Fishing the receiver up with the cord, yo-yo bonk to the forehead. "Annie? Annie?"

"Arnie?"

"Annie." Her voice sounds like herself.

"I'm worried about you, Arnold. Get help."

"Annie. Annie. Don't do this." Shit. Ribby dog whine. Toss me a bone. "Annie, you still there?"

"None of us is here for long, Arnie. I'll pray for you. 'When those went, these went; and when those stood, these stood; and when those were lifted from the earth, the wheels were lifted up among them.'"

"Please, Annie."

"Warhead," she corrects.

"Warhead, please no chapter and verse. Just talk to me,

Annie. *Annie*, talk to *me*."

Her sigh conch-whorls in his ear. "Oh, Arnie. When will you learn? There is no *me*. There is no you, no Annie. 'Even as a fig tree casteth her untimely figs, when she is shaken of a mighty wind.'"

"Frig the figs. Okay, no nobody. No more prayers though, huh? Just don't go, Annie. Don't hang up."

Whispers.

"What? I can't hear you." Imagines her palm muting the phone like a trumpet.

Hisses. "Can't talk."

"What?"

"It's lights out, Arnie."

"Jesus, listen to yourself. Dormitory of doom and gloomers. What's next, Annie? Parietals for pessimists? Well, we have time for a burger and a shake before God's shrapnel strafes us into flesh-ribbons, but what's the big dif?"

"Arnie, I have to go."

"Wait. Wait. I'm sorry. Just joking. Remember jokes? How many white horses does it take to screw in a light bulb? How may Beelzebubs to rotate your tires?"

"Arnie."

"No, but seriously folks, where you all from? Jerusalem?"

"Arnie."

"A lot of Jerusalemites in the crowd tonight."

The phone coil's a stricture on his neck. "Yeah, Annie. Same old same old. World's ending on October twenty-second, year 2000. Here today. Gone tomorrow."

"No. Arnie, I mean it. Zeke's going to put a tracer on the phone."

"Zeke." Body snaps up. Coil constricts like a boa.

"Annie."

"Ack."

"He's serious, Arnie. You're violating our civil liberties. Freedom of religion, Arn. It used to mean something to you."

"Dn. Don."

"What?"

"J'z minit." Saint Jude in our time of need, ignore us. Freaking phone garrote.

"Arnie?"

Loosen that Windsor knot. Hopeless causes. Hack. Sound like a pervert breather.

"Arnie, are you okay?"

"Yeah, I'm okay; you're okay. Not. Don't lecture me, Annie, about freedom. You're slave-dancing for some apocalypse-wow huckster, and you're lecturing me about liberties."

"Arnie, don't."

Annie's voice again. Foot in the door. Wedge in the pie, sweet molasses Shoo-fly pie. "Annie. Just come home. No get with de-program. No agenda. Just you and me on Halloween. The downtown scene. Grown-ups playing dress-up. What do you say, Anna-banana-split? I won't mention the Righteous Brothers, I promise. No cajolery. No tomfoolery. No skull-duggery."

"Arnie. You're always so glib."

"Glib? Why that sounds like a Smith word, sweetie. One of those tony film seminar words."

"Arnie."

"I could pick you up. A proper date. We won't even see the housemother. A peck on the cheek, a check on the pecker."

"Arnie, I have to go now."

"Say 'yes.'"

"Arnie."

"Maybe. Say 'maybe'."

"Arnie."

"Maybe."

"Maybe. Good-bye, Arnie."

Stares into the receiver. Maybe? Kisses its mouth. Maybe. She said maybe. Maybe coming home. May be home for Halloween. Hope. There's hope. Hope to beat my gorilla-muscled chest. Well, ding-dong, King Kong.

I admit that I am powerful. I apologize to nobody. I take it one lifetime at a time. Step one: hope. Step two: crack the door. Step three: fiddle-de-dee. Step four: Warhead no more.

Annie's pillow. Annie's undented pillow. Hey, pillow, you listening to me? I'm pillow-talking to you. Annie's coming home. Get down, you goosefeather mama. Annie's coming home. Briers, thorns, and scorpions, be not afraid. My sleeping beauty's coming home.


Crouches into his denim jacket, shearling pile collar, yanked Elvis style. Pillared Compound looks like some ante-bellum bughouse, slashed with black paint slogans, letters dribbling all over themselves like nursing home words: Repent. The end is here. Silence in heaven the space of half an hour. And to the angel in the church of Philadelfia . . .

Philadelfia? Judgment junkies can't even spell. Get thee to a dictionary. The curse of an oral culture. Recursive progress. Postmodern primitivism. And Annie-knee-socks, my Chestnut Hill shabby genteel cucumber sandwich is in there?

Come on, Annie, show thyself. Come on, girl. I am calling you by telepa-communications. Get on the synaptic internet, honey. Your Arnie's here to rescue you. Come on down.

Wait, there's the door. Just two ghouls in brown caftans. Hello, Papa Cass. Damn, staring right at me. Hunker down, Arnie. Old boo eyes is lasering you. Well, hey. It's hard to look inconspicuous in a cherry red convertible. Yo bro, you know the old saying, Never trust a prophet with a Porsche.

Wait. There. Behind the monks. Two pin-up girls in pinafores. Hard to tell with the shorn locks. Goldilocks? Annie?

Popping up like the Pillsbury dough boy.

"Annie. Annie. Hop in. I'll take you for a ride in the country."

Eyes downcast, averted, demure. False modesty, Annie, does not become you. I've seen you scream and quake. Annie in ecstasis. Thighs clenched. Head thrown back. Mare eyes rolled to the whites.

"What's with the Buckingham palace bit? On guard. Come on, sweetie, look at me."

Head down. Then, "Arnie, look out."

Hey. Hell-o. Ten-ton dumpster humping up out of nowhere. Brakes. Brakes. Comin' atcha. Brakes.

"Annie." Spine's made out of rubber, bobbing my head like a spring-necked novelty dog, trying to get her attention through the passenger window, Annie's window. "Annie." She's looking right into my eyes. Annie eyes, peacock blue, fanning, iridescent.

Annie disappears. Thor does a Dracula imitation, spreads his brown winged robe.

"Get thee behind me."

Annie moonwalks behind the sackcloth. 'Pay no attention to that man behind the curtain. I am the great and powerful wizard of Id.'

Tune in the Peter Lorre voice. "Yo, Drac', I vant to talk with the veer-jin maid. Heh, heh, heh."

"Twelve-stepper Warhead has shunned the sinners of the old life and is preparing for the end." Omega sweeps Annie on.

Cut the corner, ding the bumper. What the hell, insurance already over the top. "Annie, please." Her eyes, cowled. The brothers huddle. Come on, Annie. Look at me, baby. What's the use? "Annie, I'll call. I'll call you, Annie."

Downshift and squeal, rubber zippers on the pavement to close the gap between my Annie and me. Eat my dust, monks.


Feel like a hollow-core door, low as low-grade carpet. 'Can't bear the condo anymore. Baby boom gloom and doom: the luxury of a broken heart and home. Annie's absence omnipresent.

The cacti are dying of dehydration. Sing it Otis, "I need your water. I want your water, but the well run dry." Place looks like it's decorated by some Banana Republican on angel dust. Annie during her jungle fever phase back when we were negotiating the pre-nup agreement. Never even got to the nuptials.

Maybe, go out. Have a few Manhattans, chat up hose models. But I'd just end up spending the night watching their lipstick wear off. Not Annie. Bazillions of women in the world, and only one Annie. God has a cruel streak. A practical prankster. A lapel boutonniere: stop to smell the roses and it squirts you right in the eye. Loss is always specific. Right now, Camus could cheer me up. Annie everywhere, Annie in the couch, Annie in the bedroom, Annie's diaphragm, goddamn, still in the medicine chest.

Don't even think about turning on the radio: Annie air waves, crest after crest, and I'm in the trough. All pop songs are about love, love failed in a million miserable ways. "My baby's joined a millennial cult. She jilted me, and it gave me quite a jolt. I wilted like the Wandering Jew. Now I'm feeling like a dolt, cause my baby's done joined a millennial cult." You're killing me, Annie. I'm a dead Elvis. Cilla? Cilla? That you, honey?

The phone is the most alive thing in the room. The phone has connections, umbilical cords. The phone has hope. No messages for you, Bub, except this: Arnie, you are A-lone. Big time. The last lawyer in the universe with no one to plead his case to.

Clink the cubes in the glass. Your Dewar's profile: lint in your pockets, urine stains on your boxers, whole room smelling like shot elastic. Here's to you and self-pity, Arn.

Glass splashes to the floor. The phone. The phone. Scramble. Hustle. "Annie?"

"Arnie, you need to take a searching and fearless moral inventory of your behavior. Stalking, Arnie? Honestly, Zeke is threatening an injunction."

"That polyester suit, that fruit in a leisure alb is threatening me? I'm the best in the biz. I'll paper him all the way to injunction junction."

"He's serious, Arnie. He wants you to leave the Compound alone."

Shift gears. Wrong tactic. "Listen, Annie. I don't want to talk about Zeke the geek. We've got hard chatter to do. You and me. Annie, I want to get married. No pre-nup. No pre-condition at all. Just you and me. Together. Get a little center-chimney cape. You can play house, dress like Martha Stewart, wear pink espadrilles, dance the lobster quadrille, anything you want, honey. Your movie. You're the star."

"And the name of the star is called 'Wormwood'."

"Annie, leave the Bible for Gideon. You're talking to old Arn here."

"Arnie, you just don't get it. 'So I will send you a famine and evil beasts, and they shall bereave thee; and pestilence and blood shall pass through thee; and I will bring the sword upon thee.'"

Slump onto the hassock. Feel like a sock who's lost its partner in the all-night laundromat. "Anna-banana-peel, I'm on my knees. I miss you. I miss your dopy snorking laugh. I miss your morning breath. I miss that tiny scar on your pinky finger. The callus on your elbow. I miss your Cajun blacked catfish even when you set off the smoke alarm. I miss your Apple Brown Betty, your tuna noodle hotdish, your toast. I even miss your toast. No one makes toast like you, honey."

"'The fathers shall eat the sons in the midst of thee.'"

"Annie." Voice makes me jump. Lower the volume, Linda Blare. Where in hell did that come from? "Annie?"

Silence.

"Annie?" Stare into the black hole of the phone.

"Yes. Listen, Arnie. You could get yourself into trouble here."

Whispers.

"What?"

"Zeke's got a temper. A bad temper. And other things?"

"What? What do I care? What's the hold, Anadama? You fucking him or what?"

"He knows about you. He saw you."

"Gee, I'm quaking in my wingtips."

"Arnie. I'm trying to tell you something. Ezekiel knows things. The quake, Arnie, the big quake."

"Yeah. The quake." What now? Plate tectonics?

"Ezekiel saw it in a vision. You can't keep secrets from Zeke."

"Okay, Zeke speaks. Let's talk about you and me, hon."

"The sixth seal, Arnie. The quake was the sixth seal. The L.A. riots? Think about it, Arnie. The city of Los Angeles."

"Los Angeles?" Narcissus and Echo.

"Los Angeles. The angels."

"What the fu--? Spanish 101? Yours is the prettiest piglet, Miss. Repeat after me. "Señorita, el porcino de usted . . .""

"Arnie. Don't clown around. 'One third part of the trees burnt up and all the green grass burnt up.' It is prophesied."

"Yeah. yeah. And Nostradamus foretold the Juice's verdict. You're talking to a lawyer here. There are no big truths. No justice. No final judgment. It's just spin doctors spun out of orbit, Annabelle. There's only you and me, Annie, the way we were." Shit, if I start singing, "Memories" I'm sticking a gun in my mouth.

"Ezekiel doesn't like you hanging around. It's that simple. The Compound's private property."

"I'm just an innocent bystander. I didn't trespass, lass. Listen, I'll cut you and Zeke the freak a deal. He sold insurance; he'll buy it. Just one night with you, Annie. Just spend Halloween with me, give me four, no five hours to just be with you, I swear on a stack of redacted Bibles, I will never bother you or the Compound fractures again."

Pause. "I don't know. I'll have to run it by Zeke, first."

"There you go. You do that, Annie. Then have his bubba call my bubba. Feature it, Anna, you and me. Halloween. From All Saints to All Souls, sweetie, we'll let our spirits soar. What do you say? The way we used to be."

Little Annie wistful: "Arnie, there's no turning back."

"No turning back? Great Gatsby, doll baby. Don't kid a kidder."

"Good-bye, Arnie."

"Au revoir, cherie."

The Zeke-mobile, a converted hearse yet, fins up to the curb. Wouldn't even let me pick her up. Afraid Cinderella's going to turn into a pumpkin. Old Arn in the condo door, Peter, Peter, pumpkin eater, waving at Papa Omega.

"Don't sweat the small stuff, Bela. I'll have her home by midnight."

Bela's spooking around the car to Annie's side, bows. Petite conference. Okay, and they're ready at the gate.

"Annie. Hey, Annie." Jesus. What is she wearing? From little black dresses to long black veils. Jesus. Here she comes, Miss Apocalypse.

Armageddon Annie in my arms. I've memorized these bones, that dip in the small of her back. The baby powder smell of her skin. "Annie. Annie. I want to see your face." Raise the veil; your bridegroom's atremble. "What? What happened to your face?" Into the klieg light of the streetlamp. Holy Hollywood. "Annie?" Tilting her face, her pretty pointed chin into the light. "Anna?"

"It's me, Arnie. It's just makeup. We put it on for Tenebrae."

"Tenebrae?"

"It's our funereal ceremony."

"Who died, Annie? Aside from the shale deposit which gave its life for the cosmetics?"

"We're all dying. Mourn for the world."

"Let's mourn inside. I need a drink."

Ushers her inside into the tribal love nest. Hands shaking, E.T. meets DT's. Phone home. Points the scotch bottle at her. Annie, alien Annie, shakes her head.

"We do not drink. I humbly ask him to remove my short-comings."

"Well, I'm just a ghoul who can't say no." Upends the bottle. To hell with the glass. Where is Annie's face? Can't find its contours under the green and black and saffron grain. "What's with the makeover?"

"It's camouflage."

Green reddens her eyes, boozy, puffy like she's been on a millennial binge, a millennial crying jab. Affect nonchalance. "Camouflage?"

"It's part of our ritual preparation for the end."

"Ah. So you, what, expect to blend in with the vanishing rain forest? Have the wrath of God pass over a clutch of middle-aged mutant gonzo turtles?"

"It's symbolic." Annie adjusts her black veil.

"What exactly does it symbolize?"

"Our willingness to return to the natural state."

"Natural state?" Swig that sucker.

Turtle head nods, explains, "Nothing."

"Well, that natural look does nothing for you if you don't mind the fashion statement."

Not a word. Not a blink. Looks tiny in her black tent. Tiny in the living room of jungle pelts. Where is her face? Where are the hollows beneath her cheekbones? Where is the tiny dimple which punctuates her mouth? Every crease and wrinkle filled with grease. Her face a forest floor, a contour map of mustard, black and moss. Dabs of light in dark places. Her face shedding some squamous second-skin. Her face an under-growth tangle of dark and light.

"You're making me uncomfortable. Please stop staring."

Approaching her, arms careless, bottle dangling. "Sorry. Just something of a new look for you." Lowers her veil. "But, hey, I'm starting to like it. Just takes some getting used to. Is it true fronds have more fun?" He brushes his palm over the pale blonde halo. "Your hair." One lock, a pig's tail curl around his thumb.

She flinches. Steady girl.

"You always had such beautiful hair."

"Remember the deal. Proper date. Twelve o'clock, and I'm home."

"This is your home. Here. You bought this couch. That's your hassock, remember? Your clothes are still in the closet, your lingerie still in the drawers."

She shakes her head. Strange reptile smile. "Arnie, I'm not the woman you used to live with."

Grabs her wrist, wanting to hold her in place, tether her there. Annie twists her hand. The twin tigers of her braceleted tattoo stare at him.

"This is a joke, right? You're going to say any minute, 'Just kidding, Arnie?' I was just getting back at you. The pre-nup? The one too many Mai-Tais in the Aloha lounge. Welcome to Hawaii, Arnie. Every boy just wants a lei."

Annie stares at his shoes.

Nothing, nothing could be worse than her awful silence. "Come on, Annie. Say something. Laugh. I always made you laugh."

Eyes lacing his shoes. Wills himself not to parallel her line of vision, but, shit, just can't help himself. What's so interesting about his shoes. Strange they look to him with her eyes, soles with tongues, souls with tongues. O solé mio.

"Annie." His fingers trace her cheek. Can't bear her face. The face on her face, green reptilian lips, Apoca-lips, twin snakes in the Eden of our love. North and South of Eden. Arnie, old man, can you kiss those lips? Pass the endurance test of love?

Glimpse of her tongue curling so kitten pink inside those orthodontic works of art. Busses her cheek. Air-kiss of death. Closes his eyes and, dizzy, swoops. Tastes like grease and Annie, Annie. Thump in his chest could be his heart, but it's Annie, screaming Annie.

"Without are dogs, and sorcerers, and whoremongers, and murderers and idolaters."

Tears rolling down her face, green and yellow tears like a sloppy paintbox, striping her face, pink and Annie. Candy Annie. He kisses her tears, her cheeks. Grease paint smudging his hands.

"Woe. Woe. Woe."

"Whoa," he hears. "Whoa. Okay, okay, baby." Bumbles love-sick to the medicine chest and knocks over the diaphragm, fumbling for cotton puffs, baby oil for sweet baby. "Comin' honey."

Annie's standing on the camel woven into the killim rug, face a bleary work of abstract art. Crying but she's smiling, mouth an inverted rainbow. What's she smiling at? Wacka-wackadola.

"Aw, honey." Murmuring. "Aw baby." Soothing as he strokes the lizard skin off onto the oily cotton balls, dropping them on the hassock. Always hated the hassock anyway.

"Honey," kissing the pink shells of her ears. Drops her black veil to the floor and lifts her, carries her into the dark bridal doorway of the bedroom, rests her on the bed. Kissing her face, her downy hair. Rehearsing the curve of her neck. His hands defining her thighs, her hips, her breasts. Her body a gnarl of muscle. "Aw, Annie. Relax." Her breath on his neck. Her breath, closer now. "It's okay, Annie."

Doorbell buzzes. Buzzes.

"They'll go away." Buzzes.

"Answer it, Arnie."

"They'll go away."

"Answer it. They'll egg you or soap your windows."

Buzzes. Fly in his Coke bottle head.

"Arnie. Go."

"Okay. Okay."

Kicks the hassock. Bruise on the shin for sure.

"Trick or Treat."

Toss a galaxy of Milky Ways through the storm door. Ooh-wee. Nobbing with the goblins tonight. The woman clothed with the sun. The beast with seven heads. "Stay there, Annie. I'm coming right back." Put a stranglehold on the scotch bottle, dowse the front light. Quick check in the bathroom mirror. Face like a depressive finger painting. Who *are* you? Holy mother of God. "Just a minute, honey. I'm just washing up." War paint on the fingertowel. Annie's judgment day cosmetics using my face for a smudge pot. Crumples the towel in the sink. Flush the porcelain god. Gargle. Garg. "I'm coming home, honey."

Annie still on the bed like a patch torn out of the night. A small, dark, quiet thing. Strange to me. Feels so tiny. Her wrist bones like wishbones in my fingers. Moaning, "Woe. Woe. Woe."

Jesus. She's praying. My knee between her thighs, and she's praying.

"He that leadeth into captivity . . ."

Hush now. My fingers on her mouth. Safe now. It's all right. Her face wet and glistening in the dark like a puddle on a parking lot. Small orange glows from the condo crime light rising like moons in her peacock eyes. Eyes fix me with love or something like it.

Annie. Annie. Moaning.

Her black robe bunched into the hollows of her hips. Annie praying. "And the spirit and the bride say come."

Come. Come. Her tongue tastes like barley malt. Come. Come. Come on now. Come on. Pushing in between those Annie thighs. To die for thighs. My Annie. Following Annie down the dark street, down the dark hall. Annie up the stairs. Annie on the landing. Oh, Annie. Oh, oh Annie bliss. Baby manna, honey. Love: the bright and morning star. Reach to do the afterglow little glow worm. But Annie?

Then the light is on, throws everything into stark high relief. Annie white faced, mouth miming a grin. Her black robe hemming her feet. She towers, looms over the bed, a thin black line.

"Good-bye, fornicator. I'm going home."

Arms spring wide like calipers. Snap closed on the tailwind. Annie's shadow. "What the?"

Naked. Dick shriveled, a shed snakeskin. "Hey." Following the robe. Nude and ludicrous. Knees, knobby and scaly. Arms, white and hairy. "Annie, what are you doing? Where are you going?"

Awful hyena grin. "Revelation, baby. That's the deal. I'm homeward bound." Taps her tattoo, impatient, as if it were a Rolex. "Kee-rist, that Omega's always late."

"Annie. Don't be ridiculous."

She's wrapping herself in the black mantle, a wedding gift for the dead. Twin eye-beams poke into the atrium window as the hearse glides in.

"Trick or treat, Arnie," she says. "I admit to you the exact nature of my wrongs: I cut the deal for Zeke. He made me the Alpha female in the Compound. I didn't want to go through with this. I never loved you, Arnie. This is the twelfth step. The last one is always a doozy. Carry these messages to the others, Arn. Sayonara, baby." Floats the last word like a twisted lemon peel.

Staring at her black back, voice a hand on her shoulder yanking. "What is *this*?"

"This is the way the universe ends. Not with a bang, Arn." Palms a Milky Way as she exits. Drops the wrapper on the floor. Annie, a door slap.

Arnie listens to himself in the third person, listens to the bang of the door reverberate for eons. Bang. Bang. Bang. His heart is an echo chamber. His bare feet root to the floor. Dry, his mouth, as salt. He is as naked as a whimper. He is the sound of one hand clapping for the tree, applauding its soundless pratfall into a forsaken forest.

# HOW THE UNIVERSE WORKS

## (MODERN FABLES) I.

"Daddy, Daddy, come quick. The chicken fell down the well."

Dumb cluck, the farmer thinks. But what to do? His daughter is weeping. His wife twists her skirt in her hands. "For God's sake, do something."

"What can I do? It's a chicken, for Pete's sake." He looks at the lowering sky. "All right," he mutters. He stares down the well. It's there all right, splashing, its wings, frantic. His daughter screams.

"Help it. Help it."

"Just shut up," he says. He stares at the rope. Should have covered the damn well years ago. His daughter screams. "Shut her up," his voice echoes out of the well. Tiny splashes. He tests the rope. Might hold. He drops the rope, hears it lash into the water. "Just stand back. I'm going down."

Hand under hand. The well smells like moss. The stone is slimy. Steady. Easy. Hand under hand. The world above disappears into a circle of dark sky. Their voices tumble down the shaft like dark birds: Hurry. Save him. Hand under hand. Holy shit. A freefall. A scream. He plunges into icy water. Something wrong with his leg. What did he hit? Feels like something tore, but he thrashes anyway back to the surface, hears their voices hollow, large like they're emanating from his chest, the voice of God: Is he okay? Are you okay?

"Yeah, yeah." Where's the fucking chicken? "I've got him. I got him." Grabs him as best he can, thrusts him up and, damn, if he doesn't fly, fly right into the gray circle of sky. Far away, his daughter cheers. Okay, now what? "The rope's broke. Get a rope."

"What?"

"Get a rope. Get a fucking rope."

"A rope?"

"My leg's broke. Get a rope."

The gray circle falls silent. Where are they? What the hell are they doing? Leg hurts like a son-of-a-bitch. Tries to grab the side, but, damn, it's slick. "It's cold," he hollers. "It's cold down here." Thrashes. "Are you there?" Squints upward at the circle of sky, but it forces his head under. Where are they? "Hurry," he yells at the hole in the darkness, but it's looks smaller now, like that circle at the end of cartoons. Th-th-that's all folks. His teeth chatter -- cold or pain. Come on. Oh God, not for a chicken. A hero for a casserole dish. A rope drops. It dangles halfway down the cylinder. He can see it snake-like sway and curl. He swipes at it. It's too high, way too high. It rocks back and forth like a pendulum. "It's too short," he yells. "Hurry." Time.

"What?"

But he has no voice left. "Too. Short." Can't breathe. Under again. Stone strikes his head. The small circle closes over him. No. Oh no. No. Yes...

Above, the chicken flaps, shakes water off his wings, clucks contentedly.

"I can't see him," the wife says. "Are you okay."

Are you okay, the well answers.

The daughter screams, "Do something. Help him."

The wife runs back and forth erratically by the well. The rope slips and lands with a splash. The well is silent.

"Help," the daughter screams at the sky. "Help."

The wife stares into the well. "John. John. Don't go. Are you there?"

The chicken, dry now, looks at the girl. What was all the fuss about? "Whew," he says, "that was certainly a close call. Well, I've got bad news and good news. First the bad news."

The sky snickers; it loves a good practical joke. The chicken grins, clucks. Now the good news, the chicken crosses the yard.

"Oh God," the woman screams.

The mouth of the well is silent. And the chicken lives happily ever after.

## II. LIGHTNING STRIKES

We are sitting in the Union Street bar telling lightning stories.

I read about a blind man in a storm who was struck because of his metal cane, you know. So, he's standing there beneath a tree and he's struck, but the cane grounds him, and he recovers his sight.

No shit.

God's truth.

Imagine.

I am.

Well, I read about this guy who's such a golf fanatic that he keeps playing the eighth hole even though this terrific storm's whipped up, see?

Jesus, must be pretty dumb to hang onto a putter while all hell's breaking loose.

Hey, think about Ben Franklin.

No thanks. You think about Ben Franklin.

So, the guy's wiggling his fanny, getting ready to hunker into a nice swing and bam. He's hit.

Right in the old plus fours.

No, it struck the club of course. But get this: guy gets a hole-in-one. And after he's struck -- he's bald as a cue ball; I forget that part -- his hair starts to grow again. Gets a brand-new full head of hair. Talk about electroshock therapy.

Full head of hair, no kidding? Hey, you could market that. Can you see the infomercial? Don't wear a rug, cut one, zap, with golfer's instant sod. Grows like a fucking Chia pet.

Damn straight. Hey, you guys know how turkeys drown. They drink rainwater but forget to swallow, so they drown.

That's why they're called turkeys.

I got a lightning story, but it's kind of sad. Friend of mine got struck seven times.

Seven times? You kidding me?

Nope. Seven times.

Must be some high risk there. Was he a tree cutter or something?

Nope. Sold insurance. Nice guy. Struck seven times.

What happened to him?

He couldn't hack it. Killed himself.

Killed himself. Gee, that seems sort of extreme. Couldn't he have just come in from the rain?

Hey, you guys know how turkeys drown?

# A GIRL, A CAR, A BAR

A martini in a conical glass. The girl's phone rings. She has been reading perhaps or folding laundry. "I'm coming over," he says.

She is excited. She is anxious. Again, again they will fight or fuck. She throws the laundry onto the floor of her closet and presses perfume onto her wrists and waits for the voice to arrive.

A black car fins into the parking lot of the bar. A martini in a conical glass. The man taps the counter, stares at the door. In a dusky apartment, a girl waits. Evening falls or rises.

The phone rings, startling her loneliness. Hospitals, police. A car crumpled on the side of the road. "Where have you been?" she screams at the phone. "Where were you going?"

A girl, a bar.

A martini in a conical glass. The voice calls a girl. "She will never find out. Let's meet at the bar." But the girl, the other girl, never arrives. The sun sets in the bar, in a conical martini glass. A black car spins out of the parking lot intent on meeting his girlfriend, the one who waits. An accident. What? The rest is conjecture.

A bar. A girl sits alone. "You could do better," the bartender says sympathetically.

"But I was late." She talks to an answering machine on the pay phone. "Where is he? Why didn't he come?" She is angry, then worried. When she leaves, she rolls sadly down the highway, humming softly to a radio tune which she didn't realize she knew. On the shoulder, blue lights spiral neurally. Busy men strobe in the darkness. Jaws of life. Jaws of death. Some poor shmuck has smashed into a tree. The air bag blossoms out the shattered windshield.

A girl. A bar. A car.

She parks her car. When she enters her apartment, her phone is ringing. "Yes?" she grabs the phone. "What happened?" But it is a girl's voice screaming at her. She knows who it is although she's never met her. She hangs up the phone and pours herself a drink.

The girlfriend gets into her car and drives to the hospital. She wants to take care of him. She wants to yell at him. She is shaking with worry. She wants. She wants, she suddenly realizes, none of this. She eases the car onto the shoulder, U-turns. She wants a drink. She pulls into the parking lot. The bartender is on the phone, mumbling to his girl, "Poor thing. Stood up. Made me realize how much I love you, baby. Yeah. Me, too."

A martini in a conical glass. The stem is blue. She thinks how we have this one life which is why, perhaps, he wants to lead two. Why can't one do, she thinks. The man on the stool next to her fiddles with a matchbook cover. He will flirt with her, invite her to his place. In some order, in some pattern, it all goes on and on.

A drink. A phone rings. Somewhere there is always a girl, a

girl at the other end, another drink, a temporary safe or unsafe place, and in between a car that thinks it knows where it is going. Accidents intervene. Life intervenes. Love is a form of folly and loneliness the cure.

The girlfriend orders another drink, another. She lets the man light her cigarette. She calls the hospital on the pay phone. Her boyfriend yells at her, "Why aren't you here? I need you."

He needs too much. She stares hard at the man on the stool and, without deciding, decides to leave alone.

A girl. A bar. A car.

The car noses the double yellow lines. Parallel lives. Lives split and twinned. Double vision, just more of me to love or loathe. Blue lights twist and twirl in her rearview mirror, glance off her forehead. Mind on overdrive, she squints, too drunk to feel dread. She pulls over, unrolls her window. Cop. He leans in. She can smell his breath. He is too close. "Miss, you were driving erratically." He sniffs. "How much have you had to drink tonight?"

"Just a couple."

He nods. He explains to her that she does not have to submit to the test, but if she declines, automatic revocation. Words. Blue lights.

She nods. She cries. I can't. DUI. I need my car. So humiliating. It's just. My boyfriend, see?

Then his face shifts. She sees the change, the glimmer of lust. Maybe cut a deal. Open the door, honey. Slide over.

Can she do this? She hears his zipper. Can she do this? She discovers she can.

Later, she wipes her mouth. He tastes toxic, like ammonia. Clots in her hair. She hears the zipper again. She is still crying. Okay, she says.

Okay, he says, now get in the back of the squad car.

But you said.

Get in the back. Her wrists ache as her arms twist backward and he asks if she's resisting.

But, she says, but.

She hears the radio crackle. She drops her head to her knees.

## FEMALE CAUCASIAN WHITE FORD ESCORT

How the world works. Too weary to feel shame or pain or indignation, but it would be so lovely to be surprised. She stares at the cage between her and the cop, the world a tilt-a-whirl of lunatic light. Blue. A blue stemmed glass. A perfect cone. A mesh of bars between parallel lives.

A girl. A car. A bar.

# CASSIE BUNYAN'S YARN: A SHORT TALE

E veryone loves a love story, and ours was a ripsnorter. How we met? My sister, Mary, fell into the river and was swirling toward the falls. I ran back and forth, screeching so loud that it rained Canada geese. He must have heard me, because there he was -- a fine, strapping man as rugged as a granite outcropping. He just hefted up a boulder and threw it overhand and dammed that river as calm as a pond. Then he scooped Mary out and set her on the bank.

How could I say no to a man like that. I fell like a tree, and nobody yelled, "Timber." He grinned at me, and I felt pretty in his eyes. What was I wearing that day? My skirt that I stitched together out of twelve Hudson Bay blankets, and the blouse that I fashioned of a clippership mainsail. I curtsied and he grabbed me like a man who was used to getting his way. His arms were as sturdy as oak, his thighs as hard as tree trunks. His eyes glittered as blue as his ox's coat. That was that.

Paul hitched Babe, born in the winter of the blue snows, to the St. Croix Road, and she tugged it straight, and at its end Paul built the bunkhouse which was seven stories high. Our bedroom was on the top floor, hinged, so that the moon could pass at night and we could lie in each other's arms and watch the stars crinkle and glint, whispering and baby talking to each other until we fell asleep, our words freezing in the winter and thawing in the summer, so that June swarmed with sweet words as thick as bees on honey.

The year of the two winters was cold, colder than the blue snows, as cold as snowsnakes, so we let the reversible dog sleep with us, and sometimes Babe the Blue, and the Teakettler. The children came, Teeny, my daughter, and Jean, my son. Paul was often off logging. He'd logged his way from Eastport, Maine, where he'd rocked in an ocean cradle, all the way to Minnesota, laying a corduroy road as he chopped along. He was a natural with wood. He logged North Dakota for the Swedes, and then he logged Alaska treeless. Pawky, he was and inventive. He invented the two-man saw, and the grindstone. Always inventing.

When Paul was off logging, I wasn't lonely. Chores filled time. I cooked chicken and pancakes for Johnny Inkslinger and the other lumberjacks. Paul invented the rollerskate so that I could serve the men quickly before the griddle cakes froze like the chimney smoke. I designed a coat-of-arms out of spruce gum and baling wire for the bunkhouse, which figured Babe. And I gardened, once raising a cornstalk that grew to heaven and burst into a popcorn blizzard. Teeny and Jean had a stockpile of snacks that saw them through seven years. I split logs for the woodstove, and I could repair just about anything with one of my hairpins. I was busy. Darn tooting.

When Paul came back from logging, he always brought a buffalo or two back home, and ladders of salmon from the river. We ate well. And we loved well. Those were the happy years.

But after the spring that came up from China, Paul started ranging farther and farther on his logging trips, designing the

Grand Canyon, and rivers, and lakes. The intervals between his visits home grew longer, too. The children were grown and gone, and I found myself alone too often in a solitariness that stuck me as sharp as a cant dog, as piercing as a peavey.

I consoled myself for a while. What could I do about Paul's wanderlust? After all, he was a legendary lumberjack, off doing what legends do. Legends become themselves. But my days were blue and wintry, and my bed had become enormous, enormous even for me. My thoughts tilted and jumbled and crammed together in a logjam. I no longer had anyone to cook for or sew for, and I wondered what had all that hubbub been about? Where had the years of serving gotten me? The cooking, the cleaning? Where had the time gone? And where does it go exactly? Are all those days and months and years heaping up somewhere out there in the forest drifting against the gnarly trunk of a pine like quiet snow?

When Paul next returned, he was not himself. He told of another logger down in the southern lumber camps, Tony Beaver, a pretender to logging legend. He needed, Paul said, to reinvent himself and for forty days and forty nights he did nothing but stare at the woodstove, stare until there were bores in the cast iron through which the lambent firelight stared back, like yellow wolf eyes in the moonlit woods. I was losing him, I knew.

On the forty-first morning after his return, Paul had worked it out. He said that he was going to see Teddy Roosevelt about some new inventions he was planning: the motorcycle, and the telephone, the refrigerator car. And he had this notion about irrigation. His mind wandered, and he followed it. What could I do? Men wander. Women abide at home. Women abide.

After Paul invented the telephone, he called me to say that he was going hunting with Teddy on the "River of Doubt." I knew all about the river of doubt. I was drowning in it, just as surely as Mary almost drowned on that morning when I met my lumberjack. But he was a lumberjack no longer. He was changing and changing fast, and I wasn't certain that I liked the direction of the change. Paul Bunyan, industrialist? It wasn't natural. If this was his direction and the direction of the country, then I worried for him, for it, for its destination.

Paul sent me a Teddy Bear. The accompanying note read, "Speak softly but carry a big stick." Odd advice from a legend. So, he had become a champion of deceit? A sneaky pugilist? Even Teddy had a heart; he spared that bear cub after all.

And what had become of my old bear of a man, my Maine woodsman with hands so woodworked that they had grain, my husband treetop tall? He had diminished for me. I had time, too, much of it. Every day I sat and thought and sat and thought, perfecting loneliness. I knew now what a stump feels after the woodsman fells the tree. I was as low as a log in a skid. In the slash.

The problem with legends is that they might not be true. Legendary wife, I began to feel apocryphal. But I was as real as Babe with her horn span of forty-two axe handles and a tobacco plug. I do exist, I told myself. I am not simply an old wife's tale. I whistled for Babe and she lumbered over, and I patted her between the horns. I, too, was Babe the Blue.

I saw Paul one more time. He came home to tell me that he was headed to Texas, going to become an oilman, a wildcatter. I looked at him as hard as he had looked at the old woodstove. "Oil?" I said. "So, greed is it now, Paul? Have you gone greedy?" Where Paul walked, the country followed. I missed our unhinged night-time sky, the whispers of pine trees, and the lyric of the stars, the wide, wide expanse of this country. All diminished now. No horizon, any way you looked. Paul left, and I discovered that I no longer missed him.

I knew what to do. I whistled for Babe, my preposterous ox,

and I hitched her up. We headed north and we are going to walk there, walk and walk through the tangy pines and the blue and mournful snow, walk up the purple slopes and beneath the star-spangled sky, walk until there's no more north to go. And I'm not looking back, not once. I know what happened to Lot's wife. And I am no longer Paul's. Paul's wife. I walked right out of legend, a tall tale, foreshortened. Cassie, I speak for myself. If you see a large woman and her old blue ox making their way through the forest, let us pass. Please let us pass.

# VERMONT TRILOGY

## CITY OF GRASS

I t was two tramps in mud-time who started it, Green and Green. Green said to Green, "You're brown as mud." And Green said, "My name is mud."

"Mud," Green said. "Very interesting. Rhymes with pud, and spud. Chew the cud. Udderly ridiculous. Fud. Bud. Luddites lugging luggage with the duds. Hmmm... Very interesting. It flees in so many directions."

"Flies."

"If cows could fly."

"Precisely."

"I mean when cows fly."

"Precisely."

"I mean purple cows."

"Precisely."

"Purple cows could fly."

"Never seen one."

"Precisely."

Green and Green walk to the green. It is white. It is winter in Townshend. Paul Auster is not on the green. Willie Nelson is on the green but not in Townshend and not in plus-fours. Willie Nelson is in the wings of the charity fund-raiser and trying to explain to Bob Dylan (that is not his real name) the Zen of golfing. Paul Auster (and that is not his real pseudonym) is in New York (and that is not in France).

Green and Green arrive at the white green. There are no cows. The cows who are not there are cultic cows, private, arcane, even obfuscatory. The cow whose name is not Auster moos, Guernsey.

The cow whose name is Guernsey moos, Jersey.

They are confused cows, or misnamed, or doppelganger cows, William and Wilson, who are green in their parallel lives, cows with the milker's black veil over their eyes, cows who are cowed by their own inability to imagine themselves into Townshend let alone into Paul Auster's (that is not his real name) imaginative ability to overlook them even as he writes the Greens where they will graze.

The cows which are not there are somewhere else. Only a Still Man could find them. An urbanite man, however, urbane could not find them. They are sub-urban, rural. They are Townshendite cows.

Green and Green are still on the green wondering what brought a cosmopolitan to Vermont to write a book that will show no trace of the setting in which it was composed.

It is summer. Paul Auster is in Vermont. The farmhouse is in Vermont. The author is in the farmhouse presumably writing a book with no cows. His daughter is flying down the stairs in a shaft of sunlight from the etched glass panel windows. He is manipulating a detective through a gameboard maze of elegant ideas.

A detective could, perhaps, locate the cows.

No one could locate the author; he is in New York. Or perhaps Paris.

## II. SPOOKS

If animals have spirit energy as we presume people do, then hordes of ghost cows haunt the hills around Townshend. They low, and moo, and boo, bemoaning the coy dogs and savage winters which have made them spirit cows. Herding, they huddle beneath the windows of the farmhouse. But no one pays them any mind. The urbanite smokes a cigarette. He mistakes them for fog. The only thing easier for an urbanite to overlook than a cow is a cow spook. They stamp their spectral hooves, huff their phantasmal breath. They stampede. They are, in some sense, mad cows.

No one remarks it. The farmers are gone from the hill. The daylight is drained from the sky. The author lights another cigarette and stares out the window. *Too much nature. Too damned quiet.*

*Mrs. White with the candlestick in the library.*

## III. THE LOCKED ROOM

According to Alberto Manguel, Paul Masson, horrified by the paucity of Latin and fifteenth century Italian books in the Bibliotheque Nationale in Paris, devised a list to remedy the catalogue. He invented all the titles. When Colette protested the use of imaginary books, he responded that he could not be expected to think of everything. But then, he already had.

The author is lining his shelves with imagined books. The author is writing imagined stories. Stories made of ash. One huff, and they're gone. Up in smoke.

A girlfriend told me this anecdote: she is in Paris for the summer. The bookstores everywhere feature Auster.

She mentions this to the bookseller.

Oh, yes, he says, Auster is very popular here. He is so French.

I met him, she announces. He's a contemptuous poseur.

The bookseller winces. No, no. He is very shy. He is my friend.

She pauses. Oh yes, but his real name wasn't Paul Auster.

I am in a locked room of ghost books, imagining Paul Auster in Vermont. He is wearing red and black plaid, an orange eye-smarting down vest. He is switching home a herd of spooked cows. Paul Auster is in Vermont, but not vice versa. Does where we compose inform what we compose, or do we always write in locked rooms? The cows ruminate or stroll, seeking Auster everywhere -- Auster in the grass, Auster in the muck, Auster in the trough, Auster in the stanchions. No Auster.

Paul Auster is hitching up his overalls. He removes a pen from his bib. Outside, Vermont is brooding so quiet that you can hear the sap drip. But he doesn't hear it or the lows of the insubstantial herd. There are no cows in Paris. He listens to other voices, locked rooms. Fanshawe waves goodbye. Bossie, bossie until the cows come home. He comes to the last page just as the herd is heading out.

# I MARRIED YETI

I know what you're thinking. I used to think that way myself. I'd go slumming for love at the redneck bars, *The Rainbow Room* or *The Stumble Inn*. The more tattoos the better. Anchors aweigh on some well-flexed bicep. MOM throbbing on a pectoral above a thumping heart. Men who mistake slurring for sweet nothings, belches for conversation. They couldn't be too primitive for me. Squinting in the shade of their NRA caps, hulking in their sherpa-lined denim vests. Their faces tanned, their boots pinching their sulky feet. Trailer treasures. I, too, used to think that they had the corner on lust. All that raw animality muscling its way out of a sleeveless T-shirt. *Stella.*

That was how I fell for Sasquatch. I was jogging on my lunch break. He was thrashing around in the foliage, foraging perhaps. Who knows? Small talk wasn't his strong suit. But he loped out of the bushes, looking perfectly unevolved. The rest is history. I brought him home.

He had great eyes. Wilding eyes with furtive yellow tapeta. He lurched around the kitchenette, spilling sugar, guzzling beer, knocking over chairs. Major and minor appliances bit the dust. The mayhem was thrilling. He ripped off a cabinet door: foreplay. I chased him around the still upright dinette set. I tried to corner him, but he flipped me to the floor. On my back I thought, Now. Oh boy. Some like it rough. But he had just found the pretzels. They sprayed over the room as the plastic split. I like a man with appetite. Some things are worth the wait.

And he had great hair. He had hair like Kansas. There's no other way to describe it. So, I waited until he settled down a bit. He and the pretzels nestled into the couch. The TV was on, Talk Soup, I think. He was mesmerized, so I just let him zone a while, habituate to domestic life.

It wasn't ideal. He didn't seem to know that I even existed. It was like having a hassock for company. But I could bide my time. I brought him beer nuts, corn chips. Crumbs littered his tufted fur. He grunted his contentment and nodded off, farting in his sleep. The spider plants wilted. The walls shuddered. But I was patient. I'd tamed a few in my day.

The first few days were the hardest. There were problems. Those big feet. His feet kept arriving early, surprised, twelve inches before he did, on a collision course with all vertical surfaces. Like clown shoes. Desk chairs, table legs, couches toppled before his feet. He lurched and lunged and trundled and slouched. But I was used to that. I'd dated before. I let the furniture fall where it may, the decor become horizontal.

And he needed a shave. He needed a shave righteously. I'm all for stubble, but there are limits. His was hair with a grim purpose, hair with a plan, hair trying to colonize my condo. Still, I didn't want to rush him into a clip, a trim. Even with Big Foot, one step at a time.

On the fifth day he turned to me and said, "Stone soup. Talk Radio. Sharon Stone."

"Darling," I said. We were making progress. But not much else.

On the sixth day I picked up a case of pork rinds on my way home. The condo was a shambles.

"Utah Jazz," he greeted me, grabbing the carton.

"Oh, baby. Oh, oh baby," I said and righted the couch. I found the broom beneath the dinged Maytag. The TV blared. The pork rinds sifted over the room. He breathed a deep sigh that sounded like love but it could have just been a crush.

I swept up the field mice and dead sparrows and corn chips that fell from his fur. The room smelled like scat and dead men's closets and wet clay and flat beer. His scent, his alone, raw to the bone. Playfully, to get a rise out of him. I poked him with the broomstick. He stood up. He was massive. His head punched a hole in the sheetrock. With a furry hand he grabbed me, tossed me into the kitchenette. "Harvey Keitel," he grunted.

In a swoon of love and a litter of pork rinds, I asked from the floor, "Do you think that there's too much violence on TV?" No answer, I was moving too fast for him.

I stopped jogging during my lunch break. I was getting enough exercise peeling myself off the walls and floors and moving his big feet so that I could sweep up the litter of chips and pretzels, the occasional fruit bat. A small maple tree was rooting behind his left ear. He needed pruning, but he hadn't advanced to grooming issues yet. The courtship was still young.

He learned to use the phone. "Pizza, pizza," he said. The empty cardboard boxes raised a skyline behind the sectional sofa. Things were looking up. He cuffed me with affection when I came home. We still had not consummated the relationship, but there were signs of crescent tenderness. To help me when I swept, he shifted his feet, his awesome feet (and you know what old wives say about feet). And he let me prune the sapling. But there were setbacks, too.

That mishap with the neighbor's dog. Who would have thought that Bandito's bones were so little. Not much meat to a Chihuahua, I imagine. But missing links will be missing links.

But I was still missing something, something more than links. The night after he polished off Bandito, I confronted him. "Where is this headed?" I asked. "Do you see any future, you know, for us? As a couple? I mean, how do you feel about me?"

He buffeted me to the floor. He said, "Drew Carey. Parkay. A senseless tragedy."

I grinned up at him from the carpet of partially eaten corn chips. He was doing the Lambada to a Taco Bell commercial.

At last, I had an *in*. I started teaching him to dance. We twisted and shouted to Elvis. "Are You Ready, Teddy?" Only I sang, "Ready, Yeti." I don't think he got the pun, but the boy could cut a rug. He was clumsy at first. Those feet got in the way. But then he found the beat, the step, the Mashed Potato, the Pony, the Boogalo, the frenetic Funky Chicken. He was break-dancing the furniture to smithereens, and I didn't give a hoot, because he dipped me, double-dipped me, took me for a spin. Soon, I thought. But I should have seen trouble coming.

On Fat Tuesday I came home from work with paper sacks full of onion rings blotting with grease. "Bigfoot, I'm home," I hollered from the door.

He stumbled toward me and finessed a bag. He popped an onion ring on my thumb and grinned. "Rob Petrie," he said, "I love Lucy."

"Wilbur," I whinnied, but I was worried. Then he kissed me. He tasted like minty mouthwash. He tossed the onion rings out the window. He prepared an endive salad. With balsamic vinaigrette. And croutons. I was suspicious.

There were other signs. Perky new Provencal print curtains above the kitchen sink. The broom back in its closet. The floor swept. He started losing weight and hair. Gobs of it, mats of it decorated the sink, clogged the bathtub. Every knife in the house was dull. Every disposable razor disposed of. He stopped slouching. He began to look pink and rosy, expectant, that look that boys get when they begin wearing deodorant instead of sniffing their armpits.

Then one day it happened. I opened the condo door and there he stood, nattily bow-tied. "Fred Astaire," he said.

"No, no," I yelled, "say it ain't so. Gene Kelly maybe. Baryshnikov, okay. Nureyev, even Frank Sinatra on the town, but not Astaire. Not Fred the Suave Astaire."

But it was too late. He was boneless, elegant, even glib. Every hair slicked into place, every move a grace note. He tapped his spiffy way across the spic and span floor, extended a hankied paw. What could I do? He was effortless, effete. I lurched. I reeled. I grunted. I fell to my knees and sobbed. I tore my hair. What had I done? I'd made a man of him. There was nothing left but to show him the door with the sorry realization that primitivism is but a thin veneer over civilization. Too tame for my blood.

"Begone," I said, pointing him the way. "Begone you benighted berry-picker." No hunter and gatherer he. Ignoble savage no more.

He executed a grapevine, a glissade, and a triple spin.

I covered my eyes.

"Dust yourself off and start all over again," he crooned hopefully.

I covered my ears. My heart was hardened. I removed the onion ring from my thumb and flung it, I know not where.

"Baby, you're the greatest," he pled. But it was too late for that now.

"To the moon, Sasquatch." I shoved him. He was limber. He tapdanced across the room.

"And darken my door no more," I said, slamming it.

I was not without regret. I suppose he was just warming up. He could have brought the house down.

From the window I watched him, expecting to see him singing in the rain on the sidewalks. But he lumbered, hunched down the crime-lit street, diminished into the night back to where Bigfeet came from. Did he crouch somewhere in the silage with a group of his peers, yarning in Yeti-speak, "You won't believe what I saw. I don't believe it myself. I hardly know what to call it. Smallfoot. This short, hairless, pink scrawny thing, but a biped just like us." Did his friends ridicule him?

It was quiet in the condo, no crunch of tortilla, no flop of foot. I flicked on the tube. The movie channel. W.C. Fields spluttered, "It ain't a fit night out for man nor beast" to a bucketful of snow in his face. The sadness hit me full force then. The upholstery still smelled slightly boggy. His scent. His alone. I smelled a memory of him dancing the *The Monster Mash* with an upholstered chair. Perhaps he'd turn around. And meanwhile I could gather up the clots of his hair and weave a welcome mat, a big place for him to wipe his feet if he came back. Bigfoot, come home.

I missed my missing link as we can only miss what goes away. I counted the days. He didn't come back. I counted the days and ways I loved him. But still he didn't come back. How could he *not* know, the big lug, that I was game, that I was game for anything.

# AND THE VOICE OF THE TURTLE
# IS HEARD IN OUR LAND

C ody's toeing his authentic, imitation snakeskin mail-order boot in the dust, kicking up tiny tornados because Amanda, his lover, isn't wearing underpants again, and she's just mounted Dumbstruck, the white mare, and is trotting restlessly, her denim skirt bunched around her hips as she posts, unnecessarily close to the horn on her western saddle. Pawpaw, the sixteen-year-old stablehand gapes, standing behind her, the reins slack in his grip, his interest raising a circus tent pole in his baggy pants.

Amanda's red hair tickles Dumbstruck's arched neck as she peeks over her shoulder at Pawpaw. "You coming?"

"Shit," Cody says. "Unreformed slut."

Pawpaw, who doesn't talk except with his hands, buzzes like a bottle fly and pole-vaults onto Fly-by-night, the pinto, holding her in check about a velvet muzzle behind Dumbstruck's flank, so he can watch Amanda's pretty ass gallop in the saddle.

"Total slut," Cody says again, because the memory of plowing Amanda six inches into his mattress as she rubbed the skin of her calves off on his stubbled cheeks, the tang of her red hair, the nips of her teeth puncturing his bottom lip, the careless sway of her breasts as she leaned over his wash basin, splashing the thicket of her crotch is but an hour past, fresh and yeasty still. Her sweet and musty scent, nutmeggy as a glazed doughnut, still sticks to him. "Total tramp." He punts a pebble.

"Yes," Big Bill, Amanda's husband, agrees, "she's special." Big Bill pats his stomach, squats in the dust of the corral, and teeters his back up against the split-rail fence. He tosses a handful of gravel, considers the random lie of the spray, plays "connect the dots" with the rocks to see what emerges. He reads omens in their accidental contours, a relatedness like that of stars configuring constellations, whose contours he has a predilection to find in the stones: two prongs, a tailed goblet, a parallelogram, Taurus, Virgo, Libra. What do they signify? The bald observatory dome of Big Bill's head gleams. He rubs it for luck.

Cody grumbles and cinches tighter the bandana on his thigh where he tucks his buck knife. He flinches. "You don't get it. You're old and fat. But I balled her righteous all night, right side up and upside down and sunnyside and over-easy and far side of the moon. I did her pretty, until I lost count and consciousness. And she's already off poking her butt up in the air for the next sniffing rabbit hound."

"Yup," Big Bill grins. "Amanda's generous with men." He grunts as he jacks himself up. Standing tall as he's wide, he urinates against the fence post. He studies the damp pattern his piss action-paints in the dirt. Another star sign, the joined legs of Gemini, one leg slightly bowed, the other tapping its foot forward, poised to Lindy-Hop away from its laggard doppelganger. The twins. But what does it mean?

Cody rubs his bristled jowls, chafing at the remembered

rawness of Amanda's calves, vigorously striving to raze the thought of her. "There's no satisfying that slut."

"Oh, she's satisfied," Big Bill says. He doesn't bother with his gap-toothed fly. Many doughnuts ago, the press of his fat separated the zipper teeth at the base. "You might even say she's complacent." Absently, he runs the useless zipper up and down its track. "Amanda just loves it, loves it all," Big Bill says. "She's pure. Pure appetite. You got to respect innocence like that."

Cody whistles through the gap in his front teeth. "The hell I do," he says. "Maybe somebody ought to teach her to curb that appetite, rein it in. People could get hurt."

Big Bill's laugh punches holes in the flat white sheetrock of sky. "That'd be like pissing in the dust," he says, holding onto his bucking stomach that's jockeying, restive to hurdle off with his laugh.

Cody winces, his leg tourniqueted so tight with the bandana, his foot pings with numbing nettles. He eases the bandana knot and adjusts the sheath. "Well, Amanda might say she enjoyed herself. She might say that. She might say she was sorry for spreading herself so thin, spreading herself for everybody and anybody. She could try to show she knows she affects people." Cody fiddles with the buttons on his denim vest, drawing chicken scratches with his fingernails on his shirtless chest.

Big Bill rubs his ear. Cody's edgy, one of those people you have to watch, skittish. He can shy up at any time, spook at his own yearning for something else, something more. He never accepts what's good without a twinge in his sweet tooth for how it might be better. "Amanda's fickle," Bill says, "but she's loyal."

Regarding Cody, he slumps heavily against the fence upright. "You got a bad case of her. Snap out of it. You can't expect Amanda to start apologizing for liking to do what some inspired architect's hand designed her for. That woman is a place of worship for your cock and mine. If she ever starts apologizing, she might as well apologize for being who she is. And there's no sense in that because you've got to play the hand you're dealt. Anything else and you're cheating God, and the odds always favor the house." Big Bill squints his eyes at Cody in the hazy white light.

Cody tries to mop his forehead with his sweat-soaked bandana. But it can't hold anymore; he wrings it out and snaps it.

Bill watches Cody, waits for his anger to subside, then says, "Fate, God, or some happy freak of nature saw fit to deal Amanda a full house, to build a temple between those thighs." He sighs, pausing to think about those thighs, then comes to. "Now, let's get at it and shovel this shit before the kids start showing up for pony rides."

"That's Pawpaw's job," Cody objects, his eyes sharp as his booted toes.

"It's a job. You think everything's owned." Big Bill shakes his head. Counterbalancing his stomach by pressing hard on his heels, he turns away from Cody. Walking like a toe-less man, he heads for the corrugated tin stable. Before his five-by-five shadow slides into the bake-oven door of the shack, he's already larded with sweat.

"I still say she's a slut," Cody, who always aims for the last word, fires off.

"Finest kind." Big Bill knows Cody couldn't hit the broadside of a barn with a parting shot because his words lack wit. Pawpaw's eye-hand coordination is more articulate than Cody's aimless mouth. Bill glances up at the crossbeam supporting the crenulated tin.

There, like nylon stockings hung out to dry, dangle nine shed snakeskins, their patterns dried to diamond-point, membranous, squamous tubes. Big Bill groans under his heft and the warmth. His eyes water, shimmer beneath a heat mirage. Intuiting this is the omen he's been seeking, he blinks. How to interpret the skins? He's schooled in stars, constellated pebbles. The skins crinkle like condoms, ghosts of condoms. Bad signs, that much he suspects. He feels Cody's Bunsen burner body fuming up behind him. Something's brewing.

When Amanda gallops up bareback, Cody's leading some kid-laden ponies around the corral. Amanda's red hair, tied back with her shed halter-top, bobs its ponytail up and down in Pawpaw's happy face. Pawpaw slides in the scoop of the saddle, pressing hard against Amanda's back, his arms wrapped around her waist while his hands make small-talk, pillow-talk with the flip-flop of her unstrapped breasts. Rider-less, Fly-by-night trots behind them, the reins coiled around the horn. Dumbstruck's reins dangle their intent to trip the mare up, but like a Lipizzaner she dances, dodging their design.

With her left hand, Amanda grips the saddle horn. In her right, she balances what Bill takes to be stack of soup bowls. But, no, as the riders near the yard, he sees it's a stack of turtle shells. He grins and flags them welcome as Amanda calls, "Whoa, baby," brings Dumbstruck neatly up and dismounts with a wide-can-can kick of her right leg. She yanks the white halter-top from her ponytail and squirms into it, snarling the sarong in her long hair as it balks, rolling up on her sweaty skin. She untangles it, tugs it down and offers Pawpaw a hand, guiding his foot into the stirrup.

Big Bill trundles over to tether the mares. "You kids enjoy yourselves?"

Amanda toys with the hem of her indigo skirt and arches her back, lazily flexing her arms with a content-cat-in-the-sunshine purr. "Real good time," she says. Her sun-scratching stretch reveals the untanned half-moons of her buttocks. "We found a mess of turtle shells in the woods around the creek."

Pawpaw grins. Amanda leans over him and licks his hairless jaw with small, pink flicks of her tongue. "We got a new name for Pawpaw here," she says. "Southpaw. He's a lefty. Ain't you, hon? A wide-swipe, side-swiping lefty."

Pawpaw's left-hand balls into a fist-puppet. The thumb, dropping like a mandible, smooches the air.

Bobbing for apples, Big Bill flops his hairless head forward into Amanda's halter. With the teeth left in his head, he nibbles her right nipple. "Amanda," he mumbles, "you're all woman." He haws his head toward Pawpaw. "So, our Amanda here made you, too?"

Pawpaw adjusts the loose crotch of his Levis, his head bobbing in silent giggle.

Big Bill thumps him hard on the back. "Who'd thunk you had it in you? But if you got it in you, Amanda'll get it out. Our heavenly body," he says with pride. He tilts back on his heels, but his horse-sense whiffs some danger. Big Bill cranes his head with an effort, his neck fat wattling as he stares over his shoulder at Cody whose eyes dart white and spooky, rolling back at them across the dust yard. The snakeskins whisper. Big Bill presses his palms against his eyelids, watching the phosphenes constellate. (Cancer's crabby pentagram?) Then lumberingly, carefully, foot by bare foot, as if shod three sizes too large and fearful of tripping himself up, he pivots in the direction of the bad wind rising from Cody and opens his eyes.

Cody's lathered with sweat, glistening, outshining the ponies' wet flanks, his hide and theirs caking with a paste mixed with the dust. One of the pony-jounced toddlers screams. But his chiffon-scarfed mother dismisses him, urging Cody on. "He's just being a sissy. He's having fun even if he don't know it. He'll remember this for the rest of his life. Make a man out of him."

Cody smirks in the direction of the pink-swathed, pin-curled mother, his expression clenched to keep his face on his skull. The ponies plod round and round on their halters, ticking off dog-day seconds on the clock face of the ring. Unlike Bill, Cody's still got all his teeth, though his upper right canine's capped. Big Bill catches the glint off the cap where Cody's lip pleats up in its simper. But Cody's no longer pointed in the direction of the pink-veiled mother. Sidestepping the circling ponies with a second sight, his first sights are clearly set on Amanda where she's playing in the dirt with Pawpaw, laughing as she cups the box turtle shells in her hands before handing them to Pawpaw who stacks them, raising elaborate, crenellated towers. Pawpaw's got a light touch; he's good with his hands. Big Bill feels the angle of light shift, receives the electric buzz transmitting from Cody's gold cap.

"Don't," Bill hollers, but the yell bottles up somewhere in the punt of his stomach, because he doesn't know yet what he's warding off. The tattered snakeskins rustle in the almost-hint of breeze. Round and round, the ponies hypnotize themselves in the circle of Cody's white eyes.

"You too good to shovel shit?" Cody yells at Pawpaw, but it could be directed at anyone, even Dumbstruck, for the response it gets. Pawpaw's hands ignore him. Still yoyoing with Amanda's reflex energy, his hands twitter among the turrets of the turtle shells. Amanda smiles on the monument Pawpaw's erecting to her. She gleams in her white halter top like sloppy seconds on a too-hasty-to-pull-it-down bedspread, leans over the tower and chucks Pawpaw's chin. "I always told you, Bill, love," she says, glancing up at Bill, "it's the quiet ones you got to watch out for."

"Honey-Glazed, you could teach the dumb to speak," Bill

says, preparing to chuckle when Cody, uncoiling, breaks the gate, surprising Bill in the very instant that, sun-glint on a knife blade, he realizes this is the omen fulfilling itself. Big Bill runs uselessly up and down like his zipper, unable to close the gap between the realization and the instant in which Cody's pressing his advantage and knife blade against Pawpaw's throat to the encouraging fear-murmurs of the scarfed mama who's forgotten her son's character-building experience in awe at this more dramatic illustration of what her offspring will amount to when he's a real man.

"Don't," Big Bill says, but he throws his voice into Amanda's gooseberry lips and Yes-I-will voice.

"Don't," Amanda says. "Please don't." And she palms her hands toward Cody.

"You thankless slut," Cody says glaring into Pawpaw's eyes and seeing Amanda's there.

"Don't. Please. Don't," Amanda pleads in the whiny voice Big Bill hoped he'd never hear.

Pawpaw's Adam's apple sticks in his throat and Cody's pincered grip. "What?" Pawpaw's hands beg. "Why?"

"Don't," Big Bill says. "Don't do it. You'll ruin everything."

But Amanda does it. She drops to her knees in the dust, her skirt hiking up her brown, love-muscled thighs. "Don't, Cody. Don't hurt Southpaw, Pawpaw," she corrects herself. "He's harmless." With a knife stroke, her words emasculate Pawpaw. "Don't," she says. "Please. I'll do anything."

And as she says it, Big Bill knows with dead certainty that it will never be true of Amanda again, that her rollicking days and nights of doing anything are over.

Cody kicks at the tower of turtle shells. They clack, scatter and wobble to standstills. The claw relaxes on Pawpaw's forgotten throat. Pawpaw's eyes ungoggle. He inhales a silent chest-heaving gasp and pats the taut neck of Dumbstruck who's pawing her hoof at Big Bill's bare foot.

"Anything?" Cody demands.

Pawpaw nods so hard, his head flaps at Amanda.

"Anything," Amanda repeats, her eyes on Pawpaw.

Big Bill cries as he drumbles over to the stable to retrieve the snakeskins to start braiding himself a belt. How had he missed the signs? A total eclipse of the sun. Withers to withershins. He foresees he'll be unloading girth; he'll be needing a cinch to keep his pants on. He feels like a jelly doughnut with the filling squeezed out.

Cody stabs his buck knife into one of the upturned shells, spinning it round on the point before he pops the shell off the tip, nicking his left hand in the process. The blood pours from the base of his thumb. "Shit," he says, jamming his hand into his mouth, sucking. Righthanded, he resheathes the blade. Dust blots up the blood stains by his boots. "And cleave only to me?" he asks Amanda, feeling his desire for her ebb as she agrees. "Only to you, Cody."

Cody kicks some gravel at Amanda's knees. "Then stand-up and get into the stable. There's shit to shovel." He sucks hard at his thumb like he's snake-bit and siphoning venom. Amanda stares at the oval blood pattern in the dirt pronging two long rabbity ears.

The gauze-swaddled lady springs at Cody, plants a wet smack full on his lips. "A woman can't resist a man of passion," she effuses before retrieving her snuffle-nosed tot and rushing home to unroll her hair, and squirm into her tightest, tight Saturday night dress.

Big Bill, knowing the four of them will never be the same, busses the top of Amanda's bowed head before sagging onto his haunches to plait the snakeskins. Although standing and sitting are just inches apart for Big Bill, he feels as if he's fallen from the top rail of the fence. Amanda seems headless to him, melted down, as hollow as a chocolate bunny on a too-warm Easter afternoon.

"I told you to get up and get cracking," Cody says, returning his attention to Amanda. "And put on some underwear."

Amanda rises from her dusty prayer, brushing the dirt from her thighs, before heading for the stable. Amanda, who's rarely approached that close to danger's sparkling edge, respects the authority of its voice. She marches toward the stable.

"And shave your legs," Cody yells at her retreating back.

The snakeskins crumble in Big Bill's hands. You never should have apologized, he says to Amanda, but he keeps it to himself.

Cody, who can't shake off the veil of pink chiffon, orders Pawpaw to go shovel the shit out of the pony ring. Pawpaw complies immediately which maddens Cody. Aimless anger. He feels like a shirt turned inside out or a horse tail flicking at flies just beyond its striking distance. "I'm going to the Chug-a-lug and get drunk," he announces in a hopeful just-try-to-stop-me voice. But no one does. "And after I get drunk, I'm going to pick up that scarfed tart." His boots pinch. Sulky and lanky, Cody lopes off.

Framed by the stable door. Amanda slides on her panties and watches Cody leave. Her arms jerk up, beseeching. The naked baby-doll want of it makes Big Bill shudder. Her arms return to her sides. She says nothing. It's like Cody's sliced off her tongue, like Cody's got her penned in the corral. Big Bill can't bear to see Amanda broke in.

He trudges to the stable and fetches the shovel. Running with sweat, he digs a trench by the door. Still and straight like a corn cob, Amanda stands, staring unseeing at him as he works. Big Bill grunts as he picks her up, then lays her out in the trench. Mutely, she stares skyward as he carefully, tenderly buries her, blade by blade. He stacks the turtle shells on the mound and leans heavily on his shovel.

Using snakeskin as a tissue, Big Bill daubs at his red-lidded eyes. He tries to lizard-squint at the future but foresees nothing ominous except a long dry season. He zips his toothless fly as Pawpaw, fully clothed and whirling a riata in his right hand, canters around the pony ring, nickering and neighing, "And just think, all this time, I didn't even know I was naked."

# RED PLANETS

**M**ars' period of revolution is 687 days. My friend Jacqueline's is about one hour. She's as unstable as gas, as helium balloon animals at a kids' clown party. She's all over the place. I mean diffuse. And I am qualified to evaluate. I am an authority, a pro, an expert at breakdowns. On the job experience, I have seniority.

Jacqueline's situation. Ugly divorce. Angry husband. Lonely. Sexually lonely. Addled by longing, disabled by it. To be held, she says, just to be held. One daughter, one terrified daughter. Celia. Never enough money. Broke, in fact. But can't cut back. Her daughter needs French lessons, and dance lessons, and a nanny. What she's used to. Moved here from Portland, Oregon. Hates Boston. (Allston, actually.) Too damned cold. Expensive, too, now that she's single, sort of single, in divorce purgatory. Too alone. I may be her only friend.

My situation, my former situation? The same pretty much. Except a son, and he's older than Celia, gone now, and I am long over the longing. And unlike Jacqueline I learned quickly to live within the meaner means. No lessons except of the life variety. But Jacqueline and I have a few experiences in common. So, I listen.

Today I listened for hours. On the phone. Email, too. The computer toolbar reads, "Connect," so I do, I try. Today's problem is that Jacqueline can no longer afford her therapist, and the psychiatrist will no longer treat her over the phone. Oregon to Massachusetts. Who can blame her? That's quite a distance to diagnose.

At perihelion Mars is 35 million miles from Earth; at aphelion, 63.

Unnavigable distances. Jacqueline told her therapist about her date tonight. Now she tells me. Found him on-line -- Chuck. Chuck spent dinner spearing his steak and complaining about his father who treated him apparently like a punctured steak, rare. He said, his father said 'You are dead meat.' Then he pantomimed, screeched his chair back, and tossed the melodramatic fork to the floor while Jacqueline stared at the bowl of Pinot Grigio warming in her palms. Then he sat back down, and split open his wallet, and showed her nude photographs of his former girlfriend. Nude photographs of his former girlfriend who left him. Who left him because he was too close to his father. *I mean, who does that,* she emailed her therapist. Her therapist emailed back, *You need a new therapist, closer to Allston.*

Jacqueline tells me all this on the phone.

"What did you do?" I ask.

"I emailed my therapist again with more details about the date and asking her what she thought was wrong with the man. No more E-dating, I told her. I also asked for advice. I am thinking about having an affair with a married man."

"Any married man?"

"No, there's someone special. Specific. I mean, THE. The married man. I met him in a bookstore and wrote my phone number on his bookmark."

"Jeepers, Jacqueline, you don't really seem in shape . . ."

Then she starts sobbing. When she finishes, it is midnight.

In the mist on the green, the lithe men practice Tai Chi. The slow ballet of spirit emerging and dissolving into fog. Last week by merely looking up as I walked, I saw performers, dancers in a third-floor picture window tapping their way across the floor, top hats and canes, tails and tuxedo leotards. These scenes are not mine. They are not rehearsed for me. But they are mine, and they make me feel that life is full and lonely and unbearably beautiful. We spectators need to look up.

I am walking to work. I work. I do not have the luxury of a breakdown. Jacqueline does not work. Yet. But she is looking for a job. Jacqueline called again last night on the verge of sleep -- my verge not hers. She told me that work is difficult, that she has the soul of a poet. "Which one?" I asked. "Whose?" She didn't laugh. She told me that she's been in and out of asylums all her life.

"Why?" I asked.

"Because I'm crazy," she said.

The wolf and the woodpecker were sacred to the war god, Mars. How did that work, I wonder? Did the wolf see the bird and think, supper? And the woodpecker, that ivory-billed or red-headed delicacy on wings? Did the she-bird laugh as she flew from his lupine grin? I think that she did. I read in a magazine this week that the ivory-billed is not extinct. Neither is laughter. I laugh, I blurt with laughter as I walk alone through the morning mizzle. The lithe men do not startle.

Jacqueline and I met at Fourth Planet, the restaurant where I work. That night I was tending bar. I tend whatever needs tending -- even Jacqueline. Like her name, she is a classic. Black, jaw-length hair, lean, lean lines. But I sensed immediately that this was a woman who needed to talk, a neural buzz about her, a frazzle yearning to sizzle. "Are you okay?" I asked her.

"No," she said and in her soft voice she described the disarray that had become her life.

I offered her tea. She reminded me of an umbrella wind-fluttered inside out so that all of the skeletal braces flashed: no shelter.

When Tibetan singing bowls vibrate, Mars' melody is iron. Ferrous like Mars itself which sometimes swirls into encircling violent red dust storms. Silver represents the moon. Mars has two: Phobos and Deimos. Gold hums for the sun. Copper for Venus, paltry alms for love. If love were a hotel, mine would be named, The Last Resort. Jacqueline longs for love. About its prospects, I am saturnine. Saturn? Yes, lead. Mercury speaks for itself.

Tonight, when Jacqueline drops by the Fourth Planet for tea, her eyes are red. She has been crying, but looks beautiful, nonetheless. She usually wears black, often black lace. A pretty witch, black highlights her black hair.

"What is it?" I ask, dunking her teabag, green tea with lemon.

She slings herself into a chair. "It's final."

"The divorce?"

"No. That'll take years. My therapist. She cut me off." She says this softly as she says everything: the depressive's deadpan.

"You can find another."

"I can't. I can't she says. I can't afford one, Celia," she says, stops, then weeps. I glance around the restaurant. The manager wants this to be a fun place. Stars, satellites, moons depend from the ceiling. Glittery cut-outs constellate the ceiling. Starships decorate the placemats. An orrery twirls the planets. The tabletops outline the myths with appliqued stars. I hand her a crumpled napkin.

"Don't cry." Is this how men feel when women cry? Mingled embarrassment, helplessness, sympathy, impatience, and a sudden notion to launch like a rocket. "Please don't cry." But my pretty witch's shoulders shake.

"I'll be back," I say, and I scramble to wait on another customer.


In Brattleboro, Vermont the deacon's house has a witch's staircase, a cubist bit of carpentry that even Duchamps' futurist nude could not ascend, its intent to discourage the entrance of witches, evil spirits. We should all construct such staircases but not against witches, against sorrow. I am sad when Jacqueline leaves the Fourth Planet. But she is gleeful later when she calls me.


My father lives in Brattleboro, or used to. Now he lives nowhere at all. My last image of him? He was sitting on the screened porch in the darkness, staring at the meadow. I did not know if he was sad or happy, or what webby maze of memory he wandered. I watched him through a window from my desk in the guest house. It was a lonely image but a moving one.

Then my mother snapped on the porch light and closed the door, whether out of kindness, meanness, or unawareness of his presence, I do not know. I heard him railing. "Turn out the light. Turn out the light." Eventually he turned the light out himself. Fireflies sparkled in the shadowy night-time grass.

In the morning I drove away. On the way out of town I noted an abandoned farmhouse. A lace curtain tatted against a window with a broken pane. I did not see my father again.

Jacqueline is on the phone. Her soft voice as quick as light. She is happy again, she explains. She has found a new therapist, a healer actually, a long-distance healer.

This does not bode well.

"The healer says that she cannot treat me on the phone until we treat who I was in a previous life."

"Who might that be?" I ask.

"I used to be Vivian Haigh-Wood in a previous life. I used to be Viv Eliot. Isn't that something?"

It *is* something, but I am not telling Jacqueline what. Viv Eliot? Why not Sylvia Plath? I want to tell Jacqueline that this woman is a charlatan out to bilk her. That treating old Viv, 'the river girl,' may take some time, that this tele-huckster clearly is exploiting her hope, vanity, gullibility, pain in the name of the greed creed that now rules this country. New age entrepreneurship. But I know that her fear and pain have brought her spang to the edge, have brought her into this spaewife's claws.

"Um, how did you find this healer?" I ask.

"I saw an ad. Isn't that terrific?"

Oh, it's terrific, all right. Terrific as in terrifying. What is the measure of our human capacity for delusion? And how tender this need to believe? And what is the right thing to say to a girlfriend at a moment like this? "I've got to run," I say.

. . .

In the winter at my parents', hoarfrost decorated the bushes along the creek. In the morning the crystalline branches bristled and crackled in the sun. Cold can be beautiful.

On Mars the polar caps shrink and grow with the seasons. In the summer the dark regions grow darker; in the winter, lighter. It is summer now, and I am growing darker.

Email from Jacqueline. Tom is having his nervous breakdown now. Crystal, my healer, says that I need to start editing *The Wasteland* for him.

I tilt back in desk chair. Editing the wasteland, that's what we do. Yep.

I type back, "Where are YOU in all this?" I hit Reply. Then Disconnect. Talk about a disconnect.

My last connection? Arthur. It is difficult to love someone named Arthur. Okay, maybe not for Galahad and Guinivere, but my Arthur was not the stuff of legend. He had a tendency to crinkle his nose as if someone had once told him that it was cute. It was not cute. No one over forty should use nose-wrinkling as a form of foreplay. Ever.

Over forty. One morning you wake up and you look in the mirror, and you are old. Just like that. I moved here twenty years ago hoping to be an actress. I joined a small repertory theater. I was far too shy to act. Maybe a grip, a blackout figure flitting into the wings. But not an actress. Hence, the Fourth Planet. I own shares in the business, and I enjoy working there, but, for the record -- the whole world is *not* a stage.

We need previous lives because we cannot bear our own. In our pasts, we are always famous. Always and only famous. Always and only famous. What becomes of the obscure? In my previous life, I was myself. See? Nobody's ever even heard of me. Call me Jude. Just don't call me late to dinner.

At the Fourth Planet and Jacqueline's here, classy in her double-breasted black blazer, Catholic schoolgirl black kilt. Her voice is low but breathless, pell-mell. "Crystal says that it's about to get tough. I need to alter the fate of my past life before we can cure me in this one. I need to hide my legacy -- my poems and stories, reviews and sketches, my diaries, and letters. They, Tom and his family, want to commit me."

I wipe the counter, ask if she'd like tea. Jacqueline has never been to my apartment. Phone, email, the restaurant, that's it. It strikes me odd.

"Thanks," she says. "Crystal wants me to hit the vintage shops, dress like Viv, traveling suits and long skirts, white garden dresses. She thinks it will help me to conjure her fully. What do you think?"

I think it's nuts. How do you divert someone else's past from becoming the future that you already know that it has been, that it is. An apotropaic garden dress? "You usually wear black," I say and go to fetch her tea.

In the corner by the beverage station is an orrery, high enough up that customers cannot play with it, but I have. And I know that no planet makes a move without the adjustments, however fine, of all of the heavenly bodies, dancing partners all to the music of the spheres.

When I return with Jacqueline's tea, I ask, "Do you even know where this Crystal lives? I mean, what zip code? All you have's an area code. She might be a con man. Heck, she might be a con."

"She might not," Jacqueline said. "And that married guy?

Crystal says that it's okay to go ahead and see him. Part of healing."

I stare at Jacqueline's teacup, delicate and translucent. Swell. If hurting is part of healing.

Two nights later Jacqueline comes in with Married Guy, and he exactly looks the part. Furtive. Eyes always on scan. A big guy, verging on beefy, verging on jowly. Glasses blinkering the surveillance eyes. I am pleased to note that Jacqueline is not in a theatrical white organza tea dress. She is wearing one of her little black dresses, this one tight as a bruise. She calls me over and introduces me to Bruce who acts as if that is not his real name.

"Hi, Bruce." I shake his hand. He turtles into his button-down collar.

Jacqueline whispers in my ear, "Tom only married me for my money."

I show Bruce/not Bruce and Jacque/Viv to a table where they can twinkle like binary stars at each other from the black hole of desire. Who said there are no second acts? I am sitting this one out.

And then it stops. No dramatic entrances. No phone calls. No email. Planet Jacqueline is off on some tangential orbit and not phoning home. It just stops.

When my son turned eighteen, he moved to California, as far from me as he could get without swimming. Not deliberately. He loves me. He still calls. He is in San Francisco writing graphic novels and starting up some upstart magazine. Graphic novels used to mean, *Lady Chatterly's Lover*. Now they mean cartoons, memoir, stylization. In all of my son's caricatures of me I am wearing emotional hats, hysterical hats, hats that gnaw the scenery. I only wear hats in January. I mean, who wants to be upstaged by a hat. But it encodes something about myself that my son sees, something that I'd rather not know. If he calls me soon, I will ask him. If Jacqueline calls me again, I will tell her that Viv Eliot once told a society woman who greeted her, "I am not Vivian Eliot. She's this horrid woman who looks like me and is always getting me into trouble." We resemble and resent our missing doubles. And for their troubles, we keep inventing them.

My son called. I did not ask about the hats. Jacqueline does not call for one week. Then two. Then I stop counting.

Jude wrote "And of some have compassion, making a difference; And others save with fear pulling them out of the fire."

By the time that Jacqueline shows up in the Fourth Planet again, I am happy to see her. She is wearing a black lace top and black flirty skirt, bitch boots, thigh-high. Her daughter, Celia, wears a red and white gingham dress with a red rose at the Empire waist.

I bring Jacqueline tea and Celia a Shirley Temple. Jacqueline tells me her story. And it isn't good.

Married Guy (Bruce) left her after two weeks, left to go back to his wife, and, it turns out, HE DOESN'T EVEN HAVE ONE. This is his come-on, his sexual profile, his M.O... "He gets off on it," Jacqueline says. And she covers Cecila's ears. "Her father's going for custody." More lip-synch than speech. "And I still don't have a job."

. . .

At the end, Viv Eliot had nothing -- no passport, no bank account, no rights of identity. Not even her own clothes. In the asylum, she found none. She was not Viv Eliot; nor was she Viv Haigh-Wood. She was not.

The symbol for Mars is a circle with unfletched arrow aimed up and to the right.

Last night my son called, and I asked him about the hats. He told me that when he was little, we used to ransack my closets and try on hats to make each other laugh. Dress-ups. I have no memory of this. I do know that the universe is fast-receding from me. From everyone. From everywhere.

"Viv." I misspeak, but Jacqueline looks up at me. "You need to get a job," I say.

"I know," she says and draws a bow-shape in the condensation on her daughter's glass.

I sit in a chair at their table. "You're not Viv Eliot and never were."

"I know," she says.

Our tabletop is decorated with Orion. I play connect-the-dots and find his belt. It occurs to me that, in some sense, Crystal has healed Jacqueline.

"I might lose my daughter," she says.

I glance at her daughter who is coloring a starship place-mat. "You might not."

She smiles and drains her tea, cantilevers herself onto the boots. These boots *aren't* made for walking, and she's stilting for the door, Celia skipping beside her, the red rose bobbing.

Martian Chronicles: Helene Smith was the medium from Mars. Dr. Fluornoy conducted seances with her, during which Helene spoke and wrote in Martian. In words and word pictures, rebuses, she translated her Martian dreams. While holed up during W.W.II in Paris, the Surrealists decorated playing cards with the faces of their exemplars -- Baudelaire, Freud, Helene Smith. Helene's face is trebled, then doubled. Her hair becomes a gargoyle who hisses at her black face on which her white face rests. This image mirrors itself vertically.

Catherine Else Muller was born in 1861 in Geneva, Switzerland. She was Helene Smith.

Ferdinand De Saussure pronounced her language authentic.


I speak the language of disappointment, also authentic. I need a Berlitz class, a new language of the heart. I need a new face, another card to play. Like Jacqueline, like my son, I need to take another risk, speak in planetary tongues.

In the mist on the green the lithe men practice Tai Chi.

In the woods, an ivory-billed woodpecker makes a startling comeback.

Above stairs, the dancers tap their jaunty way across the floor.

And above them someone on Mars whispers to Helene.

# THE OCTOGENARIAN

The octogenarian, who has fallen off his bicycle, calls Caroline from his summer home in Vermont, which is just down the road from her parents' summer home. He is the father of Jack Junior, someone with whom she used to work years ago in Philadelphia. So she does the proper thing, the ethical thing, the soon-to-be doomed thing and offers to help him out. She jots down his list of necessities: olives, porterhouse steak, shoelaces (why shoelaces if he cannot walk?), triple A batteries, and a casaba melon and rings off. She walks into the kitchen.

Her mother says, "That man calls you a lot. Are you sure this is on the up and up?"

"The man fell off a bicycle."

"This is why you are still single." Her mother hefts the lettuce head in her palms like a crystal ball.

"He's Jack's father."

"Feels like a date set-up to me." Her mother gives her the oracular mother look and bangs open a head of lettuce on the counter. A spritz of water jets over the fruit bowl. "You'll see."

. . .

Caroline knocks on the octogenarian's peely paint door. The grocery bag rips and the contents spill, the melon landing plumply by the mangled bicycle propped against the wall. It is one of those sad houses with a case of Depression asphalt shingles. The lawn screams with weedy neglect. The window sashes skew into impossible angles, not right, not right. She stoops to scoop the melon from the rain-packed dirt. The door vectors open, thump, and she is staring at sudden sky – horsetail clouds against a hot July sun – a melon plugged to her chest and her demure madras skirt bunched around her thighs. Her tailbone protests.

"Got the whoopsies, I see," the octogenarian says.

At least she assumes it is the octogenarian. She is staring at sky, nursing a melon, but it is his voice. "Sorry," she says. She struggles to her knees, giving her skirt a tug down and scrambling up.

"I'd give you a hand, but I am incapacitated at the moment. The leg. Come on in."

She scurries, trying to gather the scatter. She butterfingers the batteries, bends again, trying to balance melon, steak, shoelaces, olives, feeling like a juggling orangutan on rollerskates. She follows him into the dark house, which she has not been in since Jack Junior visited from Philadelphia three years ago; it looks the same. Tattered skiing posters and art postcards tacked on an olive drab wall, a domed reliquary of a refrigerator, curling linoleum, a flea market table and unmatched chairs. Pretentious shabbiness. She drops the melon on the table. The enamel top drums.

"Do you want the meat in the fridge?"

He leans against the wall, studying her, a spindly tall man with a David Niven-ish mustache and a late late movie charm. He is wearing an ascot. No one should wear an ascot. No one, unless he is **in** a late late movie should wear an ascot.

"There you are," she says, dumping the rest of his list with a flump, a patter, a clunk.

He does not make a gesture toward his pocket, toward removing a wallet, splitting it, unfolding some bills with a crisp What-do-I-owe you. Okay, a gift of mercy.

"You can cook it for me in a moment if you would. Let's visit awhile." He gestures toward the living room, a nonchalant sweep of the arm, still leaning against the wall, and she enters. She sees.

Frank Sinatra spins on an old record player. Two Martinis (hence the olives) sweat on the coffee table, a wedge of cheese between them melting to *My Way*. This is not good; it is so not good. It's spider and fly. It's fox and goose. It's octogenarian and the good Samaritan. "I really can't stay. I have, I have appointments later, you know how it is." But he lurches in behind her, trapping her against a de-upholstering chair, and tumbles into the Danish sofa that has fond memories of the good ole days. He neatens his hair and mustache with successive fingers, pats the seat next to him. "Please, sit down." Venery agleam in his eye.

Oh mantic mother, she sees. But the poor guy lives alone. He took a fall. He's lonely.

Frank Sinatra's crooning about little town blues. She sags into the sofa but not as close to him as cheese to Martini, as far from him as the sofa permits where a coil threatens to snap her still throbbing coccyx.


Martini One: he tells her about the woman he used to live with. Recently lived with. She left a year ago.

Caroline keeps a deathwatch on her Martini. It's 11:00 A.M.

The woman was a reporter. They lived together for seven years, but she moved on and out. He shows her a picture of the reporter standing in front of a mosque, a blue scarf unfurling against her dark NPR hair. She is smiling. She is also Caroline's age. This does not bode well.

Martini two (hers.): He tells her about some twenty-something intern who works in the office of some artsy-something journal that he edits in New York. The twenty-something wore crinolines, layers of crinolines, which she flipped up when she straddled his lap and screamed, "Oh daddy, make me yours." The anecdote's vocabulary includes words like *stamina* (still Latinate), then declines to Anglo-Saxon words, solid, muscular words. Then slides to *pussy* which might purr cutely in another context. This is not it.

He chuckles and adjusts the ascot. "She was a frisky little filly."

Caroline stares at her drained (by him) conical glass. Ole blue eyes is crooning about strangers in the night. Caroline wants to frisky filly right out the door, after garroting Jack Junior. She wants to put the octogenarian under the good Samaritan's donkey, hoof him, cart him to the innkeeper's and give the innkeeper coins to throw him out.

Instead, she says, "Indeed. I really must be going."

"I thought you were going to cook for me," he says swirling his Martini lickerishly, stem between fingers.

"Appointments beckon. Got to run." She hears the crinkle of crinolines as she rises. Retro a go-go. Gotta go. "No need to get up." And she hotfoots it, goes hell for leather, beelines for the door. "Ta."

When she opens it, she stalls, stops, staring at her chariot of escape, her bright red promise of a car. The right rear tire is flat, flat out flat. She feels the air go out of her in a whoosh. There is no God. There is no Michelin Man. There is no justice in the universe. Only a farcical web of arachnid coincidence spinning her into a paralyzed chrysalis. She wants to flee, she wants to fly, but she is as apterous as a kiwi, as a kiwi fruit. Behind her she hears ole gimpy legs stumping it to the door in time to ole blue eyes. **Who** sings a duet with **his daughter?** – *Then afterwards we drop into a quiet little place and have a drink or two, And then I go and spoil it all by saying something stupid like I love you.* Who does that?

The octogenarian towers behind her in the door.

"May I use your phone?" she asks. "I need to call Triple A."


Martini three: She needs to call Double A.

Forty minutes, Triple A promises. Forty minutes tops.

The octogenarian is pulling out photo albums which feature Jackie O. on Ari's Island without the pillbox hat, the Dior suits. Au naturel. Telephoto lens, he explains, paparazzi, sunbathing. Jackie O? Jackie OH MY. "These are very rare. Isn't she exquisite?" A David Niven-ish word given the circumstances which are not good, which are de-exquisiting by each ticking second that Triple A does not arrive, whip out the lug wrench, and get her red car keeping its merry promise, tootling back to the oracular mother with sworn affidavits NEVER to doubt her again.

The octogenarian asks her if she knows how to dance.

"I have two left feet," she says. She wants to kick him with both of them. Why did her mama raise her right? She should tell him to bugger off. She should tell him to ride that broken bicycle headlong into a Mac truck. Instead, she says, "Shouldn't you eat something? Why don't I cook your steak."

"Cook my steak? Why, darling, I didn't know you cared." His eyebrows leer like Groucho Marx's greasepaint.

He resurrects himself and executes half of a hobbled waltz with a shadowy sparring partner.

She bangs around in the kitchen looking for a broiler. It's in the sink, of course, with the dirty dishes, fat congealing on top of the cold water, floating like dismal islands. She pulls the stopper. The water sucks down like a thirsty alcoholic glugging in the Sahara, and she hunts for a scouring pad. She excavates one from an archeological dig in a drain pan by the sink – rusted, soapless, hopeless -- runs the hot water and scrubs into the crusted layers, twenty layers of meals, at least twenty. Meanwhile the octogenarian Frankensteins into the kitchen, clop, clop, clop. Where are the murderous villagers when you need them? Where are the burning torches?

The Chairman of the Board is skipping in some groove while the octogenarian's ascot discovers a mind of its own, flipping like a pennant out of the collar, fluttering while its wearer explores More Joys of the Juniper Berry, Part Four.

Photographs of the reporter curl, tacked to the window next to the sink. She wonders if he has any photos of crinoline girl, she preferably not astraddle. Caroline trains her eyes on the broiler.

The octogenarian claudicates around the room, mixing drinks, plopping olives, issuing steak orders. Rare. Almost bloody. He looms over General Electric, the stalwart military fridge, glass in hand striking a pose that calculates sophistication, a stylized world-weariness, granted gimpy sophistication and stylized world-weariness as he favors the bowed left leg.

Caroline bustles, trying to look the busy, busy cook, shift him from thinking *frisky filly* to thinking *frumpy fry cook*. She stares at the red plastic wall clock over the stove. The plastic wall clock over the stove stares at her. Tick. Tick. Tick. Where the hell was Triple A?

She slides the broiler pan into the oven, cracking the door. Tick. Tick. Tick. The odor of searing meat fills the unventilated kitchen. She bends over, keeping an eye on the spitting fat.

Then he makes his move.


Martini Five: Harpo Marx without the horn.

The octogenarian staggers from his studied pose; the Martini arcs. A spritz of Martini jets over her back. The olive missiles. The glass crashes. He embraces the demure Madras skirt. Actually, he pitches forward into the demure Madras skirt.

As the Martini glass rolls back and forth on its side in diminishing semicircles, the dance begins. Caroline screams and corners the table. The demure Madras skirt hightails it. The octogenarian hobbles on. She scampers. He shambles. She scoots. He shuffles. But – truth – with each totter the old dodderer appears more limber, more supple, more feline.

Has he been feigning? He's springing around like he just invented basketball (hence the shoelaces.) It's a game. To him this is foreplay. It's a dance. To her this is mortification.

Smoke is billowing into the room from the cremating steak. Frankie is still grooving deeper into the groove with a rhythmic ratch, ratch, ratch. Music you can run to. Nice beat.

Caroline says, "For God's sake, this really must stop," as she slides past the vigilant, refrigerant soldier for the second time.

Tick. Tick. Tick. Ratch. Ratch. Ratch.

Then the smoke detector screeches on with its electronic bat-from-hell ballad.

Tick. Ratch. EEE-EEE-EEE-Ratch. Tick. EEE-EEE-EEE. Ratchtickee.

At this precise moment the Triple A truck pulls into the yard.

Like the cavalry. Like the good Samaritan himself. Like there **is** a God. And a Michelin Man.

Caroline bangs out the door, panting.

The Triple A man has on a blue uniform with his name embroidered on his pocket: Brad. She could kiss it. A wonderful name, a short uncomplicated, competent, useful, masculine name like a little nail. What were they called, those little nails? Oh, yes. Brads.

"Looks like you got some trouble in there," Brad says.

Caroline turns to check on the arson, sees smoke billowing out the door. "Oh, yes. I was just tending to it. How long will it take to change the tire?"

"Ten minutes."

She could kiss him. She really could. She races for the door. Humankind **was** kind after all.

The octogenarian greets her. "Welcome back, honeypot."

Okay, maybe not.


Martini Six: None.

The presence of Brad for some reason curbs the old goat's goatishness. He settles into the sofa and snoozes. Caroline snaps off stuttering Frank, locates a fan (in the bathtub of course) and blows out the smoke, some of it. The steak, which would now make an excellent hole-less button, she tosses out. After scrubbing the broiler for a second, she tosses that too into the overstuffed wastebasket. It clangs. To hell with niceties. She leaves the melon, the shoelaces, the triple A batteries on the table. (Hence? She doesn't even want to think about what they were for.) She washes and rinses the Martini glasses, one now chipped, and is about to creep out the door, but she can't. She needs to check on him. He is old. He is lonely. He is, likely, hungry – no redemption for that un-sewable button of meat -- and is incapacitated – doubly -- and no doubt a bit worn out by the aerobic foreplay.

She sticks her head into the living room to check on him. His eyes closed, he looks simply vulnerable. He looks like an old man.

His eyes flap open.

"Goodbye," she says. "I'm late."

He struggles to stand, ever the gentleman. "Just keep in mind," he says, "if you ever want to fuck a horny octogenarian, I'm your man."

She stares. That was certainly high on the TO DO list. She leaves.


Tooting away in the merry, cherry car, she feels free, as free as a Kiwi with wings, a Kiwi fruit with wings. But then, but then. Her hands begin to tremble on the wheel. First anger. Then an overwhelming sadness. She pulls over onto the berm.

Was this it then? Was this her future? No Greek islands for her, no yachts, no extravagant shopping forays. No one to spoil it all by saying, I love you. Just a sad old man with food stains on his ascot. A robber falling upon her, the priest and the Levite passing her by. Figmentary appointments. A date (which was not a date) gone bad.

But then she thinks of him, the octogenarian on his wobbly bicycle pedaling solitary to the grocery store to pick up his few items, pedaling solitary home, passing an evening alone with his

Martini and Frank into the wee hours thinking about the post-cards, what was, what might have been. The following sorrow of otherwise. The return to an empty house.

She had a new tire on the car, a mother waiting to hear the story. And her mother, she will not say, "I told you so."

# THE LION'S HONEY

## SAMSON'S HAIR

To be loved is a terror. Before terror, before terror gave way to horror, horror to desolation, desolation to pity, pity to lament, lament to patience, my strength poured from my sweetness, honey spilled from the blood-mangled carcass of a lion. The lovers swarmed like bees. I grew strong on the syrup of the sun; it constituted my cells, every one. I drank from a magic fountain sprung in an ass's mandible. Leeched jawbone, conjured water, the bee's comb -- that was my diet. I sprouted rare. And how they desired me, teased me, caressed me, plaited me into their brambly longings for him: the Timnite wife, the Gaza whore, and she, the traitor.

I inspired wars, deaths, treachery, lust, fear, and riddles. I was, I am, the enigma's answer. Not seven green withs, not fast new ropes. Cords frayed like flax before me. Reason, laws, constraints flayed themselves into a frenzy of misplaced want. I could not be pinned or webbed. I thrust out wildly everywhere, sleek, and vital. Men fell, and women. So many women. I held the secret of their desire. I knew how to be loved. The secret of the secret is to remain one. I loved only once, and he betrayed me and, in betraying me, he betrayed the divine. The secret of the secret is its mystery. That is the secret of all allure. That is what makes it holy. Withhold and you remain necessary: the first lesson of love. But love is greedy, will be satisfied with nothing except everything. More is never enough. Its appetite has no mercy. It consumes itself. Satisfied, it ceases. That is its cruelty.

He pampered me. Oiled me. Stroked me. Curled me between his fingers. Shining with his attentions, I lured them for him like a rare sun. I gloried in my aloof beauty. I was relentless. I parched the whore, burned the Timnite, smote the avenger's hip and thigh. Victory was my steady fare. Conquests were my spoils. For him, I cultivated a gorgeous arrogance, reveled in my beauty which outstripped the law of decency. No Philistine could comprehend the divinity of my vanity. I legitimated myself. Uncommon indecency, my purview, the anarchy of beauty, my birthright, and my sway.

When he walked, I swung, perfect, to his lope. I brushed his shoulders. I gave him every tendril of my strength. I stroked his cheek. I tumbled on his pallet. I moved to the rhythm of his nighttime snores and daytime sighs. I suffered his women. I endured their approaches. Loving, I could even tolerate his dalliances. The women came and went from his pallet. But I stayed. Honored, I could honor in kind. But love is not honor. Brutal, it demands. And when he, soul vexed to death, exhausted, and bewildered, surrendered to its riddle, it discarded him. Love riddles itself.

I loved once and once feared. I knew fear in the cornfield, the skeletal stalks rattling their husks, the singe of foxtails as I watched the army of the field transformed, rank upon rank, into pillars of fire. The charred sheaves clung whole, membranous, black, to the smut of the stocks, wicks of ash. I shivered into scalp. The smell of scorched hair is the smell of fear, is the smell of premonition, the salty smell of violent foreboding. The foxes yipped. Howled. The silence after their ululating was louder than the scattered uproar of the Philistine men, louder than my beloved's thunder. "You plowed with my heifer."

Cows. The herding dumbness. In the wind rising from his righteousness, I whiffed our disaster. He gave away his wife. Only when denied her, could he prize her. Love lays waste to its best motive. The heart is as dark as a cornfield foxed with wildfire. Why does love always pose the question: Love, what can you bear? Bear this.

He bore the gates of Gaza away at midnight. He bore the cost of thirty sheets and thirty garments. He bore the outrage of harlot honesty and Philistine honor. But deprived of the strength of my love, he could not forbear against her plots.

Love, when true, always mediates between the divine and the earth. It moves freely. In love, the dome of the temple is the entrance to the sky. Contained, love collapses. But uncontained, it curls and cossets, flies, unfurls, thickens, lengthens, vines the sky, tendrils the earth, rings the moon, raises its own dome which is a veil but not a net. Light's fingers penetrate the veil without tearing it and tat a sympathetic lace of shadow for the earth.

No love beams purer light than virgin love; it has no object but its object. Seeking no carnal bliss, domestic comfort, flattery, it hopes only to shine on the shining object of its shining. He was mine. And mine was pure. I had known no rasor. I bristled and branched, the untamed mane of my sun's son, Samson, the golden sunlike upstart whom no warrior and no beguiler could subdue.

With neither wile nor guile, I was beauty, ingenuous. I had no arms against my own power to seduce. Wanting only, I was unschooled in want, its metaphoric longing for something other, something else. The thing itself, I stared into no quiet water which could mirror me, reverse me into the simile of envy. God forgive my innocence, I betrayed him. Betrayed him twice. How could I know that being beloved, being the object of desire chops one off at the root? Seeking no carnal bliss, domestic comfort, flattery, it ensures them all. Love conjures its own paradox.

Did she, the traitor, Desire, love him? I think she loved him for a moment, that moment when she hesitated, when she knew what she had unfastened, when she understood the strength of her allure, when she understood for that one second, the one second before the awful returning power of his love, that second when she knew that he would tell her what set him apart from all men. Yes, she knew it then. But after he answered her, she despised him. He was attainable. Love shuns its own weakness.

Three times he resisted, the two of us inching, growing stronger with each resistance. Seven green withs, fast new ropes, the pin, and the web. How she admired him. How she adored him. She could not scale his scarping wind-blown pride. Then a foothold in the sand. His hesitation. Vexed, he snarled his fingers in me. There is a still moment between recalcitrance and relenting, a still moment when love is possible, is a wedge, a cuneiform opening up and out with limitless vectors, inviting everything, anything in. Something, some force like wind, responds, gets in, and snaps the legs together.

Three times a charm, but on the fourth he confided. She spurned his bed and him for pieces of silver and left him to the jackals, who, sly-haunched and flex-jawed, came slinking in. He was perhaps already a carcass before they came. I cannot speak for him. But I tried to raise the iron smell of blood in that odorless place. No smell of skin salt, of wet mouths, no smell of her following damp or his, just the smell of a sneer when she left and the smell of sand, a dry wind, and the blotting drip-dropping of time like unspilled tears or blood.

I think he waited. He did not moan or cry. He did not stroke me. No, he did not stroke me. He was beyond regret. They took him eagerly, easily, jolted his chin upward and back and slashed me. Then he cried, one cry as thin and unremarked as a single combed hair in a windstorm. The rest is in your book which forgets me.

Shorn, eyes gouged, fettered in Gaza brass, he ground in the prison house. Counting his rounds like the dark days and nights which we counted without the covenant of sight or light, we knew the bottomlessness of unmeasured despair. But the veins in his wrist pulsed. I pushed. His crown fuzzed. While we live, there's time. There's time. Time enough to count in dark rounds of blood, the stubble adorning chin, the crowning love.

It was enough for rage set between the pillars, for a rocking against the implicit betrayal of his own desire, enough to bring down a lintel and bring down, in the same wink of time in which love passes, three-thousand men and women.

And so, he raged and railed against his misplaced love, but I? I did not earn the distinction of a burial in Manvah. And I died twice and cannot die because your story, his story, deserts me. I am the ungleaned straw in the fields of neglect. I am the rain-rotted hay no chronicler gathered. Until a story contains me, I am doomed to know everything, to remain, to die and die and die without commemoration. In love's shadow and time's violence, the beloved transmutes. Only the beloved ends. The lover never ceases. The cover never closes. Tired, I wait to share my wisdom -- drying into dust on a stone floor. I, once everywhere loved, thought even the blade would love me. Cut, I shriveled into this knowledge, knowledge of the purest love. It is unbearable. It makes a paragon of its vices. It is a longing without a bottom, without sides. It stops at nothing. Restless, it is satisfied only with prolonging its longing. Its desire is always in delay. It is a terrible love; it is named Delilah.

# THEIR VOICES

S ex smells like cellars and pipe smoke and the stale sweat of old whisky. She rolls away from the memory of these smells when she rolls away from her husband. The odor has grown fainter, but it's stubborn, absorbed into her skin like glasses of whisky and soda pop kicked over on a carpet. Spills you cannot blot out.

"Didn't you hear Poppy?" their voices ask. "He asked if you wanted to go downstairs for a soda."

His hand wraps around yours. The skin feels brown and crusty, yellow as the fingertips which stub the pipe bowl.

The cellar's mustiness wells up as your feet clomp down in pairs -- his tread, heavy; yours, light. The cellar exhales soiled laundry, rotten onions and potatoes in the root cellar and the wet smell of the stacked *True Detective Magazine* cover girls, their tight, torn dresses, and tight, torn faces measled with mildew.

You want the root beer. You can taste its earthy sweetness bubbling in the back of your throat. But before he places the glass neck in your hand, his yellow-brown hands will empty you. You stall: my brother is waiting for his soda pop; let's go outside for a walk; it's too cold down here.

But his hand slides beneath your waistband with an elastic snap in the small of your back. He pulls you close into his sweat smell and whisky mouth. His breath quickens, tears him open, ragged.

Upstairs, his breaths measure themselves. Upstairs, his kisses are smaller and shorter. You watch a fat spider scurry under the washer. You long to come up for air. You curl like a question mark away from him into a dark cellar in yourself. You only know that his hand feels out of place.

From upstairs her voice calls, "Dinner," and he hands you the root beer. You clatter up the stairs toward the rectangle of light, burst into the warm yellow air of pot roast steam and their voices.

Sex sounds like footsteps in a long descent. Always you drop with faint vertigo, the tattoo of paired footfalls drumming in your ears. Over the years, the beat diminishes, but it still resonates softly like the outer ring of an echo, like a second heartbeat.

When you climb into the station wagon, he slits his wallet open with his stumpy thumb. He hands your brother a dollar bill so starchy crisp it could still be warm from the iron. He hands you a dollar, too, but your bill flags, greased thin by strangers' thumbs.

Their voices ask, "Why don't you want to go see Poppy? He loves you so much. We are going to see Poppy."

The slamming of car doors decides that you will go. But you've grown older, slyer. You befriend a tag-along cousin. When she bumps down the stairs with you, the yellow-brown hands don't slip beneath your waistband. You watch his eyes watching you; you watch his eyes wonder how much you know as you strangle the bottlenecks in your hands and, with a clink, hand a pop to your chubby cousin. He wants something from you. He wants something that you have. As long as you withhold it, you have a power. As long as your cousin is near you, he will not have it. You watch the want in his eyes churn into anger. You grab your cousin's hand and swing her arm. He wants to be the arm you swing. You smile at him; at an early age, you learn to be cruel.

Their voices remark, "How close the cousins have become. Like forefinger and thumb on the same hand." You know his blue eyes water, rain cold on you. But upstairs in the cozy yellow talk, his will cannot corner you. You relax your wiles. You can sit on his lap and let his fingers skitter tickle-mice on your leg. You can get up and walk away from him and play "Old Maid" with your cousin. You can listen to their voices resurrect the buildings on Spring Street that burned down before you were born. You can do anything except be alone. You must never be alone.

But he grows slyer, too. Sometimes he slips into the bathroom behind you. He bumps himself against you. You bow your head before the mirror unable or unwilling to raise your eyes. If you raise your eyes, he will be grinning in the glass, because he knows that you won't tell. You don't know what to tell. You suspect that what you do not know how to tell is something very wrong and very old, something that smells like cellars, something stolen and buried in dirt. He backs you against the wall. The skin on the back of your neck prickles as it meets the cold porcelain tiles.

When the doorknob rattles, he grumbles, "I'm shaving. I'll be out in a minute." He cracks the door and slips out before you.

Sometimes your skin glazes cold and glassy beneath your

husband's hands. The bed's a brittle surface. It could chip. The years temper the memory of cold tiles on your back. Your skin no longer shrivels, but it never fully warms to touch unless you lie with a stranger, someone unrelated. A part of you refuses to thaw.

When you are almost eleven, you tell your brother. His shame strikes you both mute. He touches you lightly on your forearm. The smallness and sadness of the gesture permit you to avoid each other's eyes. You realize that you should have kept it to yourself. He does. Perhaps he does not believe you.

When you enroll in boarding school, their voices insist, "You must go visit him. Poppy's paying half your tuition."

You are fifteen years old. You wear blue jeans and a striped jersey in the yellow living room. Their voices hum in the kitchen.

"Ah, how beautiful you are," he murmurs. His veiny sallow hand brushes your brown hair over your shoulder. He cups your small breast. His caterpillar tongue wriggles into your mouth.

You step back. Your eyes slap him, because your hand cannot. His head snaps, stung. You turn from him. You walk away from him, his cellar smell. Your boot heels stab the floor, puncturing his secrets, deflating them as you walk away from him. By now, you have kissed other boys, many boys, boys who taste like peach stones, boys who taste like nutmeg. Your triumph burns in your mouth like the aftertaste of his tongue -- mossy, boozy, peppery with pipe smoke. His taste keeps longer, stronger like root cellar onions.

Sex tastes acrid, rooty, used-up. The damp, gone-by, veiny sharpness of blue cheese. The edge dulls over the years. But, beneath soft, fresh lips parting, it coils there -- a small sour bud at the root of your tongue.

You have lovers. Always that first snap of elastic startles

you. When you sink into pillows, you lower yourself into a drama you hope is convincing. You descend in flights, deeper, lower, slowly pushing out roots. Root cellars, root beer. Blind male tubers sprouting on potato eyes. Albino tentacles groping cellar corners. White, webby, underground family roots. There, you forget.

Their voices say, "He is drinking himself to death." But it is taking him years. In one of those years, when they have come to pick you up at college, their voices decide to take a side trip and pay him a surprise visit. You surprise him reeling drunk. You have seen him drunk before, but never like this -- a pinwheel of arms and legs and Banshee gibberish, his legs so bowed he drags his haunches on the floor. You wish his careening confusion would spin away from you, leave you untouched -- smug, disgusted. But it only whirls you into its center. You cannot believe that he is still standing. A lesser body would cave in. His dizziness is your dizziness; no one else has touched you like that. No one else will love you like that. No one else could.

The last time you see him he is bundled into a hospital bed and a palsied vanity, stuttering, "I never wanted. I never wanted you. You. I never wanted you to see."

"He's not himself today," a nurse says, tightening the bed sheet over his chest.

"I never wanted you to see me," he says. "Me," he says again. "Like this." Drool unwinds over his cracked lower lip.

His hand reaches to the side table to reach for his iced tea. When the glass reaches his lips, it is trembled dry. Tea stains twine into his thermal blanket. From the single spots, networks of stains weave into the thirsty cotton twists dyeing the center of the blanket brown.

Sex feels like a shaking leaf. A shiver of nerves exposes the veiny lace of a leaf whose green membrane has browned, flaked off. A shudder passes through the spine, moves through the lips, through the torso, limbs, down the legs to the soles of the feet and back up the spine to the scalp. The quiver is very near fear. Over the years, the fear decreases, the trembling abates. But although weaker, the signal still transmits through your nerves, an atavistic reflex.

After his funeral, they pore over his scrapbooks -- newspaper articles, war mementos, family trees from which your name dangles like a small plump pear. When they find the pages dedicated to you, their voices murmur, "Oh, how he loved you." A poem in the school newspaper. An article on your high school awards. Another about your acceptance to college, your scholarship. A black and white Polaroid of you in bridal white, your First Communion, peels out of its ungummed corners. His hand has written beneath it: His Other First Communion. His other? As if he had transubstantiated, become you. You listen to their yellow voices. You are soil and dark corners. You are the only one who knew him, sallow hands turning fallow, the humus where rotted acorns crack, protrude their sprouting yellow tongues. His shirt cuff is dirty. Sex looks like a hand severed at the wrist. A hand, you squint your eyes against, a crawling claw groping for a body. "He really loved you."

Lust, you could accept to spurn. Love confounds you, terrifies you. Love longs for complement. His blood lurks in your veins.

Over the years that temper smell and sound, taste and touch and sight, and the lovers who, like memories, intervene, you wonder. His love acquires a newsprint label. You listen to talk-talk-talk shows. Their voices. But conclusions seem so much air. Over the years, you wonder: if your hands will turn yellow-brown, tremble like leaves, fall and fall to the roots of your family tree?

You led your husband down the stairs; he walked you back

up into the light and airy rooms and asked, "Do you love me?" And you answered, "I love you. I love him. I love them all." But someone stayed behind in the cellar. Someone is always in the cellar. When you walk alone, you will always walk in a pair.

# THE MISSING DAYS OF E.A.P

On September 27th in Richmond, having renewed my engagement after thirteen years to my beloved, my cherished Elmira, I boarded the boat for Baltimore where I hoped to gain fiduciary benefaction, advance subscription, for my project, *The Stylus*. The amatory resumption with Elmira, after such a long deferral, and my dedication to my new pledge to the Sons of Temperance, found me in sanguine, indeed almost jocund, aspect. I was embarked in a joyous new direction. Banished was the imp of the perverse. The telltale of my heart was rapture now.

I took my seat on the Pocahontas in steerage, my coffers still paltry, but I took my seat triumphally because I had every expectation that soon my fortunes were to reverse. In this good humor was I joined by a fellow traveler whom I generously acknowledged noting that his circumstances were poorer than my own, clad as he was in shabby attire, a threadbare gabardine suit with a tattered bombazine coat and stained caseinate, odoriferous pantaloons, well-worn unblacked boots, a soiled shirt lacking neckcloth and vest, and a palm leaf hat destitute of ribbon and brim. He was a sorry apparition, and his wardrobe appeared to be borrowed as it fit him not in the least well.

When I beheld this wretched soul, despite the fetor, I nodded welcome. *May God have mercy on this woeful creature.* He spoke not a single word, nor did he nod in response, so I turned my interest from my erstwhile companion to my immediate literary companion, the tales of Hawthorne, preparing to settle in for the voyage, where I forgot myself uninterrupted until my fellow traveler suddenly leaned on me.

Out of compassion, I closed my tome, prepared to be engaged in some exchange of pleasantries or discussion perhaps about affairs of the day, the Transcendalists, or the Mexican War, the famine in Ireland, the abolitionists, or the courageous work of Elizabeth Cady Stanton, but this was not his intent. Rather he whispered to me so softly that I could not comprehend him.

"I beg your pardon," I uttered.

He whispered again, and, on this instance, I comprehended him but only because I attended him more closely, leaning forward on my cane, not due to any greater effort on his part to be heard.

"Edward Allan Perry," he whispered.

A frisson tingled my spine. Had I properly heeded him?

"Edward," he whispered again, and I understood it this time as an introduction because he bowed slightly.

"How awfully curious," I observed to him. "This remarkable similarity in our names." And I introduced myself, Edgar Allan Poe. And then I scrutinized his physiognomy for the first time, due to the astonishing cognominal coincidence. I had enlisted as Perry in the army, and Allan was my adoptive surname although John Allan had foregone my adoption. I noted then with dread and a sickness at the heart, my whispering interlocutor's fine nose, pronounced brow, the mustache, trim despite his otherwise slovenly mien. I noted the phreno-logical bump posterior to his temple indicative of sublimity, the other behind his ear indicative of amativeness. But the eyes were dead, listless, brooding and subfusc. I shivered for a moment before their dullness as if death's skeletal hand had just anointed my brow. And then I laughed at my whim, I may even have laughed aloud, for my companion withdrew slightly. I worried that this poor indigent might have taken umbrage at my mirthful eruption, but he whispered nothing more. I returned to my perusal of Hawthorne, and, upon arrival in Baltimore, we parted without further exchange.

Yet as I perambulated to call upon Dr. Nathan Covington Brooks, I found myself vexed by reflection on the specter. Whispers are more mysterious than utterance, and they linger on, urgent for audience. His visage floated back into my sight and I audibly gasped, startling a passing pedestrian, as I recog-nized Perry's face as my own, fraternal images. We might have passed for twins, at very least brothers. He resembled me more closely than did my brother, Henry. As I reflected on his cognomen, I felt bereaved. Had I lost some unsuspected brother. But again, I dissuaded myself. William Wilson, fictional and pseudonymous, I was writing myself into my own tale, or it was writing itself into me. I dispensed with my gloom, and resumed my walk with heartiness, eager for the company of Dr. Brooks.

His butler courteously received me, but informed me, alas, that he was out of town. I retrieved my cane and thanked him, resumed my walk, disappointed at finding my friend out, but I consoled myself as I strolled with thoughts of my Elmira. Lines from my recent verse kept step with my gait, "She was a child and I was a child, But our love it was stronger by far than the love Of those older than we." I had only just learned from my dear Elmira, recently widowed, that her father had intercepted my letters to her when we first engaged, curtailing our courtship. She is a child, and I am a child no longer, but love, so hopefully begun, was coming to fruition at last. Perhaps Sarah unwittingly bestowed upon me a favor when she terminated our engagement because I could see with perspicacity the value of moderation and who was the true mistress of my heart.

As I navigated the streets, I considered strolling over to my old abode on Amity Street, but this seemed unwise. The streets were thronged, elections being near. As I walked, I tapped my cane, jauntily nodding to passersby who noted me. I paused to admire a Box Elder with its compound leaves, a fine old shade tree, and smoothed, I hoped surreptitiously, the black wool of my suit, less an act of vanity than a desire to be presentable, as was my wont. The suit well became me. Beneath my Elder tree, I attended discreetly to these niceties of attire, then stopped. I had the distinct impression that I was being observed. I turned and beheld with horripilation Edward Allan Perry regarding me. Had he been following me? It occurred to me that he might be a thief. Was he after my purse? I carried yet the one thousand and five hundred dollars of subscription money, part of the sum most recently procured from John Thompson. Had Perry some miscreant design?

He followed my eye, then approached me. I noted that he mimicked even my gait. What japery would this man not indulge?

I stared again into his occultating gaze. Again, the susurrus.

"Sir," I asked, "do you follow me? I really must protest."

But he only whispered again. This go-round I heard him.

"If you fear me, be aware that your cane contains a sword. You are well armed against me."

Baffled, I looked at the cane and recognized it as not my own. Ah, I must have mistakenly retrieved it from the butler at Dr. Brooks' domicile. I paused to collect myself. "Are you destitute?" I then asked, still thinking that he might be intent on burglary. But he only shook his head.

"Then I really must ask you, sir, to desist in this shadowing." And I briskly retreated with nary a backward glance.

How to amuse myself? I considered advancing to the train station and boarding for Philadelphia with the prospect of some additional editing of Mrs. Loud's poetry which would augment the subscription fund for *The Stylus*. But it seemed a shame to pass such a glorious autumnal day in the stifling quarters of a coach, so I resolved to seek other occupation.

I stopped to consider the posted playbills on a kiosk and reflected briefly that I was born to thespians. How long ago. It is odd that as one is living one's life, one rarely reflects on its plot, because the ends are so unknowable. Who might have foreseen my re-engagement to Elmira? Curious, a life's divagations. I suspect that we do not in the midst of life reflect upon its design, because its unity is not visible, endings being always obscure unlike those which we write. I quite astonished Dickens when I anticipated the ending of *Bartleby Rudge*. A novel contains the seeds which predict its efflorescences, but not so a life. In life the endings are always imminent, not immanent.

A play struck me as too brash a diversion for my current mood, so I continued to stroll, enjoying my sense of wellbeing, and noting the fine trees planted along Baltimore's bustling boulevards, the Black Willows and Blackgums, the Dogwoods and American Elms, the latter opening to the sky like bouquets.

In such a manner toward dusk did I again encounter that wraith, Mr. Perry. He had fallen into rough company and appeared more dissolute, if that is conceivable, than he had on our previous encounters. He no longer mimicked my gait. Indeed, he had a seaman's lurch and roll although he stood upon no deck. A drunkard's rigadoon. He failed to recognize me as he caroused with his boisterous mates.

I immediately suspected that he had frequented the brothels. There was no dearth of them in this seaport town, and no scarcity of rum or opium in them. That his companions were villains, I had no doubt. The shapes of their skulls, the indentations, suggested depravity. Perhaps due to my own recently curtailed proclivities, I took pity on the wretch, and worried that some harm might befall him, I took it upon myself to shadow him, uncanny reversal, as he and his companions careened down the street. Thence I followed him into a decrepit tavern.

The den was dark and peopled with unsavory customers, a gentleman with a pronounced cicatrix sat at a pub table dealing cards. A strumpet, a striped surplice over her drab gown, sat on a stool, sobbing, unheeded. The room dinned and the air choked on smoke and stale ale. I cringed and considered betaking myself promptly elsewhere, but I could not, in good conscience, desert my vigil of Mr. Perry for he clearly was not in a condition to be mindful of his own. I therefore persisted in my mission and took a safe seat in the corner from which I could survey him. I declined the server's offer of a drink, but I ordered a fish chowder by way of meager repast, for I had not eaten yet this day, being ever mindful of my straitened circumstances.

The chowder was hearty fare, and I felt quite restored after supping, but I kept ever a watchful eye on Mr. Perry who had joined the men at the Écarté table although he was clearly vagrant. Hence, he did not play, he could not play, but his fellows nonetheless stood him to several drinks, and I began to suspect that they might be coopers intent on exploiting Mr. Perry in the upcoming polls.

I watched the gamers with remorse. I, too, had once been a

gambler, and it had been the cause of the disruption with my guardian, John Allan, whose name I still bear. Drink is always a *flaçon of Du Grave*, begetting other debaucheries, lechery, and gaming. I had sinned, too, but now I sought redemption, Elmira, my sober angel. The heart will have its catacombs, but there we can put our demons' bones to rest.

It was then that the dealer approached me. "Do you have some business with me?" he asked gruffly.

"No," I answered, matching my gaze to his.

"Then why do you stare?" he asked.

"I am concerned," I answered, "about the welfare of my friend."

At this he laughed abruptly. "So that's it then?"

"That is it," I answered.

"If that is all then," he said, "may I stand you to a drink? Perhaps you would like to join us at cards."

"I am not a player," I said.

He continued to press upon me, however, to join them, to join them at very least for a drink, introducing himself by surname only as Passano. At last, I relented to his importuning and consented but only to a cup of tea, Elmira ever foremost and steadfast in my mind. After that I recall nothing.


Lacuna. I awoke in a vile room, a whore's, no doubt, my head a torment to me. What had transpired? Time was an ellipsis. I had no sense of how many days had elapsed. I dimly recalled my interlocutor and suspected that I had been dosed with laudanum. The tea. Or perhaps they had practiced mesmerism upon me such that I did not captain my own will or actions. My hands groped the bedding. The room was redolent with the foul perfume of purchased love. Only then did I become aware that I was not alone in this cramped room. A figure stood before a massive chifforobe at the bedstead's end. I startled and sat up. "Hush," Mr. Perry said -- for it was he only smartly attired now in a black suit. He spoke in full voice, clearly audible now and to every appearance sober.

"Where am I?" I asked.

"Lower your voice," he said, lowering his own. "Mr. Poe, you are, I believe, in serious danger. We are being cooped here, and I fear that these men have malevolent design upon you. Two evenings ago, they forced upon me with a pistol's authority that we exchange clothes. I have been aware of their plot for some time, and I have been following you. Elmira's engagement to you perforce requires that she forego her inheritance, a condition of her fortune unknown to you. Avarice, as you well know, sir, can provoke the most hideous plots, and such a plot entangles you now. Why I have undertaken your protection, Mr. Poe, I cannot reveal. Suffice it to say, that I knew you, sir, long ago at Bransby Academy where I incurred a debt to your kindness."

As he delivered himself of this astonishing speech, no doubt having had ample time for its composition, I noted that indeed a sartorial exchange had occurred. I was now my very double. I studied him but detected no familiarity from my youth. But time is a practiced illusionist.

He resumed, "We must speak softly, Mr. Poe, so as not to rouse our kidnappers. I suspect that they shall release us on Election Day, the third, and then enact their foul design upon us, leaving you for dead, the murder obscured by the mayhem attendant on the day. I mark the time. I must urge upon you, Mr. Poe, that these scoundrels lack all fellow feeling. You must observe my recommendations to you without question. Accept the benignity of my counter plot."

And then he fell silent. In this dark room, day and night were indistinguishable to me. On faith, I assumed that time continued to pass. Occasionally I heard banging or cries from the street below the shuttered window or from chambers below. Of even these sensations, I could not be certain.

But at some appointed moment, Mr. Perry suddenly urged upon me the transfer of our habiliments, and I complied. Had I foreseen his fate, I would have demurred.

I read about his death, my other death, in the *Baltimore Clipper*. Edgar Allan Poe, found in Ryan's Fourth Ward Polls, died in the Washington College Hospital at three in the afternoon on October seventh, 1849, of "congestion of the brain."

Nemo me impune laccesit. Except Rufus Wilmot Griswold, my ostensible biographer, who slandered not only me but also my mysterious savior, Edward Allan Perry, who authored his own death. I lived to see Griswold die and to see my former beloved, Sarah Whitman, rise to my defense. I did not die a drunkard, nor did I die of a disease. Neither did I die as a cooper's dupe. I died as Edward Allan Perry, but I also died as Edgar Allan Poe, my life no longer my own.

Imagine living to witness your own demise, interment in The Westminster Burying Ground and again in the Memorial Grave in Baltimore. Buried twice alive. I choke on it.

Why did I not return to Elmira? I am dead, and to announce myself alive would only condemn her, as I learned of Edward, to penury. No, she did not deserve that of me.

Dead at forty, I am today seventy-five years old. A vagabond, I keep my own company. The spiritualists commune with the dead, so do I in daily conversation with myself. I am the walking dead, immured in myself, condemned to life.

My putative final words? "Lord, help my poor soul." Or the popular variant, "He who arched the heavens and upholds the universe, has His decrees written upon the frontlet of every human being and upon demons incarnate." Do tell.

He who writes his decrees? What plot did he invent for

me? There is one ending. Death. That is the sole plot, and I am much enamored of it. Death is the only scribe. What a godless forsaken expanse is this life.

Today I haunt the Metropolitan Museum in New York and watch the raising of The Actor's Monument, by Richard Henry Park, unveiled by the great actor, Edwin Booth. So, I watch the commemoration of my own death. Who loves us while we live?

I have considered a leap from one of that city's elegant bridges, but I am an accomplished swimmer, trained in the James River. Dear reader, my detained Wedding-Guest, whoever happens upon this record, let me for once author my last lines, let me write a plot other than that of a sacrifice made by a schoolmate whom I cannot even recall. He died for me, and for that I execrate him. The saint left behind the sin. I am the egregious sin, my confessor. Only death absolves me. Great gloom is mine. This is hell. This is torture. Life, my penance.

*For the love of God, Montresor.* We scream into an empty vault.

*In pace requiescat* in the tomb by the sounding sea.

All words are posthumous.

Even these . . .

Perhaps I misjudged. Might endings also be immanent?

The masked revenant left three roses and a bottle of cognac. De grave.

# THE WITCH'S CURE

L ike a demagnetized needle I spin aimless days through the slack compass of summer, tat webby dreams in the dusty corners of summer houses, weave hammocks in the raspberry suckers where thrips mate their opaled beetle backs, twist dizzying skeins of you around the sharp spindles of first morning light piercing my dreams and the eastern sky. I have time to fill with my tossed handfuls of dreams, my volumes of dreams which like water, like time rise to fill the hole worn by these idly cycling summer days. Since that black winter night, my idle hands count for nothing but time. White-walled anonymous time.

That black night you were playing guitar and playing well as you always did when, scotch-sotted, you played your hand to your audience's hand in one beery bar or another. You were singing "Little Maggie" or "Rock Salt and Nails."

Earlier, we'd had an argument. I sat at a round table, my dram glass in my hand, my two booted feet on the floor. I drank Rusty Nails then, or white wine, or red, bowls of it delivered on the house. I couldn't recall why we'd fought. Like a white gum eraser, the alcohol had rubbed out the details leaving me only with the nubby residue of anger. Song by song, measure by measure, beat by beat, my toe tapped out its impatience to the end of your set so we could resume our set-to. I settled into my ire, let it filter down through cork bits, sediment in a green glass punt, the opaque lens of the bottle's ogre eye.

At the end of your set, you cradled your guitar into its case, parted company with your audience, and, while I waited for you to join my anger, you slid off your stage stool and shouldered your way into the crowd at the bar. Your turned back, the shirt figured with coyote fetishes, cacti, spurned me, transformed me from a pretty woman the guitarist's girlfriend, into a pitiable woman, a woman sitting alone, a target like a bottle balanced on a fence rail. The guitarist's shunned sloven. Fermenting in my anger, frothy, I watched you make the other men at the bar laugh, telling men's jokes, jokes about women, how women are built two-holed so you can carry them like six-packs, how they are built like bowling balls so you can roll them.

Football players flickered like cartoons against an eye-smarting field of astro-turf on the screen above you, their colored lights flitting over your heads like blurb-less balloons, like the burble of laughter following your jokes. A man's man, you charmed them. And a man's man is a ladies' man. I stared at you until my eyes fizzled fuseless sockets. My eeling need opened its horny teeth, lamprey-latched for a host to suck.

I fish-tailed toward the bar. As I approached, men's muscles tensed. I felt the twitchy beat suspended in the air, tiny, the beating of thrip's wings. Delicate tension. But no one buzzed; the men held their wingless poses.

"What can I get you, 'Nita?" the bartender asked. Craig, I think he was, the manager of The Silent Woman, but perhaps he was Edward at the other bar, Moose Lips, in Waitsfield. The face eludes me now, but he sounded like his voice.

I paused considering ladies' drinks, slow Sloe Gin Fizzes, Singapore Slings, blender drinks to drive a bartender crazy, you, too, if you had still been performing, your guitar straining to drown the silver whirr of the chopper blades, chipping ice into the white gravel of my heart. Mint Juleps, Stingers, Rickeys. The Propeller flashed through the frosted glass.

Craig, or Edward filled my hesitation with a grin. "So, what'll it be, honey? We have cock and cake, and we're out of cake."

You laughed, all of you. I laughed, too, my rotor eyes slow-turning their blurry discs back into treble-blades, the room resuming its shape, steadying, and said, "If you gentlemen can stop sucking him off, I'll take this prick right here." I laughed alone.

And they, with their flannel-shirted men's muscles, their hard chests and faces, dissolved like ghosts into the TV screen, receded dumbly like white-face cattle in a grizzled fog. But your face loomed close-up, black and stubborn as a bull's. Who could ignore such a face?

Stumble-drunk, we lurched in the parking lot, navigating the yellow, capsized cones of streetlight, yelling blind words that groped through their own steam and hovered above the snowbanks. The well-below-zero ice-bladed air sliced off my toes in my too-tight boots, stropped my torso in my too-thin Saturday-night-going-out coat, scraped my cheeks so numb, your words lost their sting and dropped like icy pebbles between our toe-to-toe feet.

"You're a freak," you screamed, waving me off. "You're a witch."

"But only on the distaff side," I answered.

"Go home." You flailed your awn-arms. "I don't want you. Leave me alone. Go home."

And I, always quick with a ratcheting phrase, answered, "It's a free country. You go home if you want; I'm going back inside."

But you'd already turned your red face from me, that one blue vein pulsing at your temple where your hair flared up, cowlicky. I followed the billow of your jacket, my eyes jumping the red and black checkerboard of your back as you gamed me in "foxes and geese," leading me inside, down the stairs again into the rathskeller.

I remember that the bartender refused to serve me, and I refused to leave. Defying whispery stares, I let my presence brew in the room. I remember you slashing your guitar strings, crooning hate ballads, your spitting teeth, a zipper-fly parting. I remember thinking, anyone who can hate me that much must love me truly, madly. As you sang, "How Can I Miss You When You Won't Go Away?", I sang, "Idiot Wind." I twisted love-knots in my hair and frizzed the circlets in the candle to singe you with the chemical burn of me. I drew snaky penta-grams in the ashes with my spittle-licked fingertip, drew char-coal manacles on my wrists.

I remember Last Call, but I don't recall my feet guiding me outside, tapping off the cold on the floor mat of my car as I waited for you to bumble out, drop your keys in the snowbank, perhaps, curse as you dug them out to drive off in your red Rabbit. My black Fiesta finned out behind you after a preda-tory pause, the head beams blinkered, navigating by moonlit instinct, by the sonar batwings of love, following my blackguard heart up and down over the glazed hills, you veering thrillingly faster and faster into the irrational curves of the unruly rural roads, me rushing into the wake of your danger, my tailgater's heart pushing beyond the hood of my car, trying to outrace the wheels' rotation, wounding the radiator in a plow-packed snow-bank, but, dribbling antifreeze, urging the accelerator pedal on, pulling up a heartbeat behind you at your green house, I knocked on your door, knowing with full-hearted, full-throated certainty, you would let me in as I called your name, "Russell, Rusty. Rusty." Three times a charm. "It's cold out here," I called, my feet crunching the road salt, the White River rushing through its ice-locked veins. "Let's talk." My fist smashing a pane of glass, twisting my wrist, the brass handle. I smiled at you, a bleeding fist of knuckles. Who could resist such love, such love willing everything right between us again?

"I'm calling the police," you said.

"No, don't." And I began to cry. My rock salt. My crescent nails waxing blood moons, dyed the white cuff of my sweater, wicked into the yarn. "I love you," I said. "Don't make me go."

You grabbed my shoulders, shook me. I thought then, for a moment, it would be all right. But you surprised me, jerked me toward the dryad-framed Art Nouveau mirror where a woman's face coiled beneath black snakes of hair, her eyes melting off her face in inky snail trails, her lips rouged with blood.

"Look at yourself," you screamed. "You're hideous. Go home."

"No, Cat," I said, my pet name for you. "You're just drunk. We're both drunk. And tired. We're overwrought. Let's just go to bed. Sleep it off."

"Go home or I'm calling the police."

"But I've come such a long way."

Upstairs, your housemates' feet touched the curious floor. Lights winked on the landing.

Your finger probed the O-hole of the rotary dial.

"No," I yelled and grabbed the cord. "Please. Oh, please." I yanked it, snapped the umbilical link like bitch from pup.

"No." And I stared at the frayed spiral of electrical arteries, red, black, and green. Delicate as threads of spun silk.

You looped the cord with a hangman's deftness, manacled my wrists with a rodeo twist. A man's man, you pushed me out the door and propped a captain's chair beneath the handle. I stood on your stoop. My bound hand five-digited a pentagram, bled its hex onto your icy step, splotching it with hot hisses, purfling the lacy crust of re-frozen snow. Blood. Salt. Moon. My elements composed a sestina to you. Ice. Blue. Eye. I howled and bayed at your window, pattered your panes with halite. You flicked off all the lights. I waited for the stars to drop a silver rope ladder. I ululated for the answering wolf in you. I sucked the blood from my scarified knuckles, offered you my colder-than-a-witch's tit to suckle. But you didn't answer.

Disappointed, dispelled, I unwound myself. I wrapped the cord tidily around the phone and left my neatness like an unexpected gift, a cat's trophy mouse-kill on the threshold for you to find.

I drove home, jagging a trail of splatters, blood, pink antifreeze, a discreet path worn in a dream-forest of half-remembered bedtime stories for you to find your way home to me.

I arrived home beneath a dome of pink light. In my barely-morning kitchen, I prepared coffee, sipped it, waiting for you to call. I watched the coffee's brown surface skim over with a milky skin like scar tissue. The white porcelain mug cooled in my hand. I watched the hands of my clock churn windmill arms, quiver compass needles, count unmeasured time as round and intricately patterned as a hex sign. But of course. You couldn't call. Your phone was disconnected.

So, I bathed and dressed, taped my knuckles. In practical low-heeled boots, I scuffed through the snow along Wales Street to the shabby florist's storefront, ordered red carnations, dozens of them, bunched into a vase. They trembled as they anticipated their delivery by winged Mercury to your white, sun-lit stoop.

Cheered by the memory of fluted pom-poms, the image of them bobbing on your steps in the winter white world where you lived in your green house beside the White River, the bouquet delivered unexpected to you like forgiveness, like unsought love, delivered like deliverance from the black hollow of longing, I returned to my apartment which waited for me, crouched, behind the hollow-core door. I waited for dayless days.

Monday bumped Sunday. Suns propellered. Moons spun. The circumferences of time radiated concentric circles. Ripple effects. Having missed work on Monday, Tuesday seemed inconsequential. Another 'Nita, or Betty, or Rose could swab the formica, scribble the orders, clip the papers up like white bed sheets for the short-tempered, short order cook to advance slowly round the carousel.

Time struck my phone dumb. Over and over, I raised its round black mouth to my ear to be certain it was still breathing its dial tone. I dialed your number until the ciphers burned like candle flares in the air, but the recording would not stop repeating itself, "Out of service at this time and this time and that." I composed words, crosswords and numerological jumbles conforming to your number. 468-5463: HIT-LINE, GOT-KIND. I watched my car mound with snow and pitied it for its handicap. Its coolant drained from the radiator; it could not heat-seek you. I counted snowflakes sifting into my drive-way, laying a soft bed for your sudden red Rabbit to warren in. I clung to a spoke of time.

I trace the unpuckered cicatrix, the bracelet, a gift from you, on my chicken-bone wrist. I smile sympathetically at the memory of its parting lips, smiling into a kiss, draining the stain of red carnations into the white porcelain of my basin before someone, perhaps you, sent someone to my hollow-core door to fetch me, or perhaps I dialed an anagram for your number, H-O-T--L-I-N-E. In the white room, in the white gown, on the taut white sheets, red circling tubes re-filled me with the tincture of gillyflower.

Now I'm here getting better, stronger. You made me everything I am today. I obey the quiet, white shoes. I drink no red wine, no Rusty Nails. I walk in straight lines in the fruit garden. I note the tiny webs of spider mites threading through the maze of berry suckers. Some spidery strands stain themselves raspberry where the thrips have thrust their straws into the ready-to-pop, ripe, berried globules.

Yes, I'm having good spells. Dutiful, I keep to my white page journal days where I write a hope chest for you, syllable by syllable, braiding crowns of cardinal feathers, dipping tea-rosebuds in paraffin, plucking fluttery petals of Oriental poppies to stuff a bed tick, dying my lips prettily with blood-root. I'm weaving my way out on a fine red thread. Spinning free. I must get free again, because -- I don't wish to be too familiar, Cat -- but, darling, I'm lost without you.

# CROW LOVE

C row preens. In sun, he glistens purple. From his black branch, Crow sees everything: the sunflowers' heads, frost-snapped and drooping like hanged men, their thousand black eyes, jay-plucked; the sparrows holding up the wire fence, the wooly bear curling on the browned-out goldenrod, rabbit capering across the stubbled field.

Rabbit loves Crow. She cannot stay away from him. She bounds to the root of his tree. Rabbit says, "Crow, you shine so. You are very handsome, Crow."

Crow holds his head carefully as if he is balancing a thimble of water on his crown. Crow knows that he is handsome. Without tilting his head, he fixes Rabbit with one unblinking eye. Rabbit, Crow knows, is furry, and soft, and warm. Crow knows things; Crow is smart.

"You think I'm handsome?" Crow caws.

Rabbit nods and her ears bristle, attentive.

"Very handsome?"

"Yes, Crow. Oh very." Rabbit is eager.

"How handsome?"

Rabbit trembles. "Most handsome."

"As handsome as Blue Jay."

"More, Crow."

"As handsome as Falcon?"

"Much more, Crow."

"As handsome as Eagle, Rabbit?"

"More handsome than anything, Crow."

Crow crows. He thinks Rabbit is very sweet. "Do you love me, Rabbit?"

Rabbit twitches. "Yes, Crow, I do."

"Do you trust me, Rabbit?"

"With all my heart."

"Would you like to see me up close?" Crow teases, arching his wings like jet rainbows.

Rabbit's eyes water. "Of course, but, Crow, I do not fly."

"I do," says Crow and, grinning, swoops from his perch, pins Rabbit by the neck, pecks her heart out and eats it.

## CROW TOTEM

Crow is stoic. His paint is peeling, but he still stares down the weather with his fierce eyes. His wing-span awns, protecting crow knowledge.

Rabbit's angry ghost scuttles like dry leaves at Crow's wooden talons. "You betrayed me, Crow."

Crow stares.

"Come down," Rabbit says. "You tricked me. I shall have my justice, Crow."

Crow is mute.

"Crow totem, even you are not above spirit law."

Crow blinks. Crow speaks. Woodenly, his beak creaks. "Do you love me, Rabbit's ghost?"

"Yes. That is why I am so angry."

"How much?" Crow asks, his wood grain softening, turning pinnate, the weather-bleached paint darkening. Crow becomes flesh again. "How much?"

"Very angry," Rabbit spirit answers.

"No, how much do you love me?"

"With all my soul," Rabbit moans.

And Crow plummets again and ravens Rabbit's spirit, leaving behind this time one black feather. "For truth, Rabbit."

## CROW NATURE

Crow loves things that glitter. Crow covets all bright things. Crow has a nest that glints with gum wrappers and gold rings, safety pins and diamonds, bottle caps and silver coins, thimbles and paper clips. Right now, Crow is eyeing a silver sports car. He thinks it is too cumbersome to carry to his nest. But Crow's hollow bones whistle with want.

Crow flies to the car and pecks at the door handle. Even Crow knows that the car is too heavy for him. But he cannot bear to leave empty-beaked, so he pecks at the side-mirror, at the woman standing in it, then hops down the silver hood, hunting a trophy, and snaps off the hood ornament in his beak.

"Thief," the woman beside the car screams, flailing with her useless scarecrow arms. "Thief."

Crow pauses in flight. He drops the silver circle on the rocks with a tinny ding. Crow hovers, stares at the woman. Her eyes glitter with gem-like anger. Crow pecks them out.

## CROW CAUCUS

The roost is crowded. Feathers whirl. Caws and croaks strangle the air. The crows argue over who will keep the eyes.

Crow restores order. Crow proposes a pecking tournament to earn the trophy eyes. Crow will guard the eyes for the victor.

Black blizzards of feathers sift down over the cackles. Blood patters. Pecked and bleeding, the birds drop, crow by crow, until one bird, battered and ragged from his effort, stands. Winking his remaining eye, he puffs his chest and addresses Crow. "Your turn."

Crow shakes his head.

The bird protests, "I pecked them all down. You must fight me now. You said that the eyes belonged to the champion."

"I lied," Crow says and swallows the eyes.

## CROW MERCY

Crow has eyes everywhere, in his stomach, on his wings. Crow hatched, alert and seeing. His eyes help him to find unguarded nests. He beaks the Mourning Dove's egg and sucks out the gluey chick.

The Mourning Dove moans and keens, "Please do not eat them all, all my chicks. Please."

"Please," Crow mimics perfectly.

"You are a father," the Mourning Dove coos, "please, no."

Crow hesitates. "Should you have left the nest?"

"No. No," the Morning Dove coos.

"And did you learn an important lesson?" Crow beaks another egg.

"Yes." The dove clucks.

"How important?" Crow chips with his beak.

"Very."

Crow's obsidian heart centers his small orange eyes. "What lesson?"

"That I should not leave the nest."

Crow sucks out the egg's innards.

"Not even for a second."

"No. No. Please. Not a second."

"You're right." Crow jabs the shells and siphons out the last two chicks.

## WOLF PLAY

Crow is lazy and logy in the sun with his fat belly full of dove chicks. Crow is dreaming of corn when his eyes open on the yellow kernels of the she-wolf's eyes. Crow's wings startle with crow knowledge.

The she-wolf grins. "Do you like to play, Crow?" she asks.

"Yes." Crow's wings are a tiny heartbeat too late.

"How much?" she asks.

Crow does not answer. In the instant the wolf clamps on his wing, Crow sees himself in the keen wilderness, in the yellow moonrise of her eyes.

Wolf loves Crow. Crow finds grace.

# THE THREE MINUTE LOVE STORY

"You're distracting," you say.

"From what?" I ask, but I know the answer: from everything, from life itself. I attract love at speed of light; it refracts before I can catch it. I bend the spectrum. My heart is an egg, soft-boiled, even runny, albuminous, the kind everyone carefully times but no one likes to eat.

You send me cards. For a week. They chronicle stealth bomber love. "Darling, hand me my gas mask." Then you inhale nerve gas. "Okay, okay," you say, "I'm sure." And we're cooking with gas.

Oh, the feeling, I remember the feeling -- mornings breaking like eggs on the rim of the horizon, white curtains billowing with light, our legs tangled, the humic smell of your shoulders, your razor cutting through the foam on your face. "Baby," you say.

"Yes," I say.

I know you by your telephone ring. It jangles my nerves. I learn the sound of your car engine, the fussbudgety way you tuck in your sweaters, the gold viney ring on your pinkie.

We spend a light year in bed eating bagels, drinking coffee, fucking each other, drinking coffee, fucking each other. The edge of the flat world is the bed. We don't stray, so we don't fall off. There be monsters there. Instead, we gaze into each other's eyes with that look that, if it had a voice, would be "Ah." We exchange little tokens. We are killing ourselves with our own cuteness. "Baby doll," you say.

"Yes."

"Sweetheart, baby, doll face, honey, cutie." Oh my, oh my.

When I fall, I fall like a tree. But if there's no one there to hear it, does it make a sound?

On Tuesday you ask, "Can I come over?"

"Over and over again," I say, over before I begin.

On Tuesday you come over and say, "I'm still in love with my wife."

"Ex-wife," I correct. But the note I red-pencil still leaves me marginal.

"Okay," I say. I want to be courageous. I'm nobody's fool. Precisely. I'm nobody's fool for love. Precisely. So why do fools fall in love? Precisely. Who else would have them? Precisely. Nobody. Precisely. Nobody's fool. But it feels so imprecise.

I know you by your telephone ring; it doesn't. I empty you from the eggcup of my heart. My mornings feel raddled and yolky, scrambled. I wish it were over easy, but it's always over hard. I am living in the age of discovery. I have discovered that my heart is like Columbus' egg. My heart is the world, and it is breaking. I want to circumnavigate the pain, but I mischart and keep running aground on the beaches of my mistaken destinations. Heart, where is your harbor? Fetch me spices, birds with brilliant plumage, gold. Fool's gold.

I dial your number and when you answer, I don't speak. "Andrea," you say.

What can I say? It's I. Men are my form of hysteria.

"What do you want?" your estranged voice asks.

Precisely. Precisely. Precisely step by step until Niagara Falls. But my mouth is full of eggshells, The Nina, The Pinta, The Santa Maria capsized in my heart. Darling, I'm drowning.

"What do you want?" you repeat. "Let's keep this brief."

"I want. I want to be. I want to be your tragic flaw," I don't say. And suddenly I am.

# THE DEVIL IN DECLINE

I t's not as if I'm out of touch. Give the devil his due. I read the signs: the chicken bones and tea leaves, the omen birds, the I Ching, the horoscopes and the cards, the local papers. I can read the lie of the doubled die: snake eyes. Seven and seventy devils in the twist of the road, my rope's come undone. Seven days and seven nights stretching end to end, spanning centuries, to fray to this, my Apocalypse: seven candlesticks, seven stars, seven seals, and plagues, and angels. I am no longer stylish. You have lost faith in me. No one believes in me, the demon lover. Spurned and scorned, I shrivel into a balladeer's archaism. Well met, well met. You make me quaint.

But I refuse to appear ridiculous. I am not going to prop myself up with sticks, stage a comeback like some old Vaudevillain of evil, hoof cloven-footed across your strutted stage, balance parti-colored balls on my goat rack, the horns of your dilemma, ride stand-up on your midnight-mares, swallow fire, belch flames, swivel my head, snap topmasts and ships in twain. Evil does no encores.

I am weary. I have walked your world, motivated your

malignancy, crouched on the chests of your virgins, crunched your babies' bones, spoken in tongues to your saints with pinwheel eyes, impregnated your rabble, toppled your cities' exalted towers, visited your stunted leaders with unholiness, gassed your masses, seduced your rib-mate, invented nakedness and sin and death. Even God took Sunday off. But there's no rest for the wicked.

My *idle* hands bore light away from heaven. I staged my own exit from paradise to live in the eternal limbo of my demesne, the prince of darkness, shuttered away in the steepled hell hole of my soul, haunted by the Babel of idolatrous voices. Without, all are dogs, whores. Yes, the devil can cite scripture for his purpose. For you, my public, I bloated with my own contagion, drank from my own fetid sewers, sweat offal from every pore, spoke with a silver tongue so forked and endlessly forked that it fibrillated, snarled, raveled, and knotted the hissy sibilant inducements which your poets so admired. Whisper softly and carry a big shtick: so, sweet poets you'll sample the susurrus of my soothing psalm; so, sweet, say you'll succumb to the sapidity of sin. Insipid patter. Putrid persiflage. The devil gets all the lines, but they snarl. They kink. The root of the stump is as bitter as mandrake gotten with child. On my throne, I brood in the palace where all past years are, desolate, a desaparecido in the most echoing and solitary of chambered souls, pondering -- where lives there a believer, true and fair?

I am not a man. I am an animal. I stared at the world through lenses of my own blood. Your filth-fisted feral child, haunches down, I dogged your lurid streets, pounced reeling into your rum bottles, teemed and beetled in the grimy corners of your gin alleys and carnival excesses, the fool of misrule.

My tail was my balancing act, the animal which gave you gravity. I teetered, bearing all your corruption incarnate. My teeth chattered with gibberish. My heart scorched a hole in my chest. My sockets burned like coals. I turned your bread green with envy, hexed your chaliced wine to pus. I webbed your charnel houses, bled in your birthing sheets, shredded your wedding gowns into widows' weeds and infants' shrouds. I made your collective backbone my home, scaled your spinal ladder and screamed myself hoarse in the neural pathways of your brain, follicle-forced beards of mold to sprout on the fruits of all your labors. For YOU. For what?

More sinned against than sinning, I ranted, raged. But poor Tom's a-cold. A weary tragedian, I've trod the boards. I've fallen my last fall. No curtain call, just curtains. I've expulsed my last gas, leered my last leer. I've retired my trident. I'll devil-porter it no longer. I'm an empty bag, a flop, a has-been, a fossil wickedness. Dismal grows my countenance and drumlie grows my ee.

You emasculated me. You sanitized my priapism. You silenced my tongue and blessed me into oblivion, a collapsed Manichean unity. But with my gouged-out eyes, I stare down your groundling world of spear rattlers, see what's transpired since you turned your back on transgression. I circumscribed sin for you. Without me, you're nothing.

Without the demon Credo, your rivers roil with blood, your towers blast into concrete scraps, your omophagic savages gnaw themselves into a feeding frenzy, your lewd daughters prostitute a pestilence, your bridges crumble, your heart pumps a toxic river and lays waste to your levees. My lunate crown mutely trumpets at your neglect, because without me, no sun. Without me, no Son of Man. I am the mirror's *tain*. The missing twin in your vampire eyes. Without sin, goodness cannot rise, and evil casts no shadow.

I, once dejected and despised, am everywhere forgotten, everywhere denied. Without me, you have no between -- only the deep blue sea. I am gotten behind thee at last, and you blunder forward into a world spun out of context until, six, six, six, my numbers roll again, dicing in the temple, to catch you like pick up sticks, like so many scattered straws and breathe sin back into your scarecrow souls. My last act could be a magic one.

Because I am your best, last chance, the savior of your savior. For HIM, for light, I dimidiated the world, assumed my half-cloak of shadow. Denying me, you extirpate the tubers of your own goodness, rip salvation shrieking from your fallow ground, snap its shallow roots like filaments of silk. Without earth, there is no heaven. Without the mountain dreary with frost and snow, no yon pleasant hills which the sun shines sweetly on.

Dirt is my element, fire, my benediction. I hallow your crimes, do penance for your virtues. I hold the scales in balance with my tongued tail. But you deny me.

Stooped and useless, doddering in the wings, I lip-read my glory days, await the cue for my second coming. Senile and defanged, an unstrung instrument of darkness, I mumble to my withered stump. Restore my potency. Make a sacrifice of my vice. Lead me to the hearthstone of hell where I may make my best bed forever. I forget myself. Eternally asea between heaven and hell, no lilies bloom on the banks for me. Oh Lord, why have you forsaken me? Forgive me **not** my trespasses. Damned to decline but not dignified to die. The hour grown long, I who never sleep, pray you, weep. Weep. Do this in memory of me.

# ACKNOWLEDGMENTS

"The Painbroker" appeared in *The Chautauqua Literary Arts Journal*; "Tenebrae" in *New Letters*; "The Corner of Dreams" in *Hayden's Ferry Review*; "Tattoos" in *The Laurel Review*; "The Unnaming" in *Colere*; "Baby, I'll be Home for Halloween" in *Chelsea*; "How the Universe Works" in *The Rio Grande Review*; "Cassie Bunyan's Yarn; A Short Tale" in *The Green Mountain Review*; "Vermont Trilogy" in *Full Circle*; 'the Octogenarian" in *Writing Disorder*; "I Married Yeti" in *The Artful Dodge*; "And the Voice of the Turtle is Heard in Our Land" in *Kestrel*; "Red Planets" in *The Journal of Arts & Letters*; "The Lion's Honey" in *Northwest Florida Review*; "Their Voices" in *The Laurel Review*; "The Missing Days of E.A.P.* in *Hotel Amerika*; "The Witch's Cure" in *The Connecticut Review*; "Crow" in *The Kenyon Review*; "The Three Minute Love Story" in *Big Muddy*; and "The Devil in Decline" in *New Millennium Writings*.

Some of the stories appeared in slightly different versions.

The author wishes to thank Paul Jones for his comments on the Poe story.

# ABOUT RUNNING WILD PRESS

Running Wild Press publishes stories that cross genres with great stories and writing. RIZE publishes great genre stories written by people of color and by authors who identify with other marginalized groups. Our team consists of:

Lisa Diane Kastner, Founder and Executive Editor
Mona Bethke, Acquisitions Editor, RIZE
Benjamin White, Acquisition Editor, Running Wild
Peter A. Wright, Acquisition Editor, Running Wild
Resa Alboher, Editor
Rebecca Dimyan, Editor
Andrew DiPrinzio, Editor
Abigail Efird, Editor
Henry L. Herz, Editor
Laura Huie, Editor
Cecilia Kennedy, Editor
Barbara Lockwood, Editor
Kelly Powers, Reader
Cody Sisco, Editor

Chih Wang, Editor
Pulp Art Studios, Cover Design
Standout Books, Interior Design
Polgarus Studios, Interior Design

Learn more about us and our stories at www.runningwildpress.com

Loved this story and want more? Follow us at www.runningwildpress.com, www.facebook/runningwildpress, on Twitter @lisadkastner @RunWildBooks